The
Gunsight Affair

The Gunsight Affair

Lauran Paine

THORNDIKE
CHIVERS

This Large Print edition is published by Thorndike Press®, Waterville, Maine USA and by BBC Audiobooks, Ltd, Bath, England.

Published in 2004 in the U.S. by arrangement with Golden West Literary Agency.

Published in 2004 in the U.K. by arrangement with Golden West Literary Agency.

U.S. Hardcover   0-7862-6920-0 (Western)
U.K. Hardcover   1-4056-3127-9 (Chivers Large Print)
U.K. Softcover   1-4056-3128-7 (Camden Large Print)

The text of this Large Print edition is unabridged.
Other aspects of the book may vary from the original edition.

Set in 16 pt. Plantin by Al Chase.

Printed in the United States on permanent paper.

British Library Cataloguing-in-Publication Data available

Library of Congress Cataloging-in-Publication Data

Paine, Lauran.
      The gunsight affair / by Lauran Paine.
         p. cm.
      Author's name appears as Ray Kelley on earlier edition.
      ISBN 0-7862-6920-0 (lg. print : hc : alk. paper)
      1. Bank robberies — Fiction.   2. Outlaws — Fiction.
   3. Large type books.   I. Title.
   PS3566.A34G88 2004
   813′.54—dc22   2004052540

The
Gunsight Affair

Chapter One

DAKOTA TERRITORY

The Merchant's & Stockman's Trust Company had not originally been a savings bank. When old Alexander Hamilton Pierce founded the institution in Sioux Falls, Dakota Territory, during the tumultuous early days, the idea had been to provide cattlemen, miners, and storekeepers with a safer place to put their money and pouches of fine gold, than under the floorboards of their shacks, or in the hollow of a tree near their gold diggings. But this wealth was only supposed to be held there, in old Pierce's stone building, called a trust company, until a bullion coach, properly escorted with either a soldier patrol or hired gun-handy outriders, could transport it down in the direction of Denver, where the government had established a mint for handling the raw gold, and where there were a number of genuine banking institutions to accept the cash deposits.

Two things changed that. One of them was when the gold petered out. A man could still make wages, grubbing and panning, but the *big* strikes were all in the past, most of the miners were gone, and nearly all the large mines had been closed for years.

The second factor that contributed to Pierce's trust company evolving itself into a regular savings bank, was the winter. There was rarely a winter in Dakota Territory where snowbanks piling up ten feet and more, could not stop traffic and transportation in its tracks, sometimes for a week, sometimes for a couple of months. The bullion coaches could not run, the money and gold sat there under the menacing gunbarrels of Alex Pierce's hired gunguards, and while it sat there its owners were required to pay a healthy fee, something they did not have to do in summertime when the wealth usually sat in Sioux Falls for two or three days, until a coach came to haul it away.

Alex did not like having to charge so much, any more than the people who owned that wealth liked paying so much, but the kind of gunguards Alexander Hamilton Pierce hired, did not work for rangeriders' wages. They were professionals.

Folks around Sioux Falls did not like having those men around, either, but there was no trouble. Alex was stubbornly unrelenting on this score; he made it abundantly clear when he hired his gunfighters, that under no circumstances were they to get drunk in the saloons, pack a chip on their shoulders around town, nor get overly friendly with the townsmen or the rangemen.

They obeyed him to the letter, but he had to pay a sizeable wage to ensure that they did.

Finally, then, about the time the gold began petering out, the cattle interests began developing more financial muscle, and the town had grown and prospered until it could actually continue to prosper without miners and raw gold, old Alex decided to convert his trust company into a genuine bank. He got a charter, organized the company, sold shares, picked a Board of Directors, hired an experienced manager named Charles Monmouth out of St Louis, back in Missouri, and, having accomplished this prestigious undertaking in a land where men still did not shave nor clean their boots, nor take off their gunbelts except at bedtime, in the normal course of their rough cow-country existence, old Alex Hamilton Pierce went out one night to sit on the porch of his son-in-law's house in town, after a big supper of grouse and mashed potatoes and black coffee, closed his eyes during the course of the desultory conversation out there with Will Billings, his son-in-law, and just plain died.

Mourning was brief, inevitably; Sioux Falls meant no disrespect, it was simply a bustling village on the verge of achieving township status. This momentum, financed and supported largely by cattle interests, but also by the enthusiasm and cash of the merchants, was more important to everyone than the passing of a man who had, single-handedly, done more than anyone else to give Sioux Falls its initial impetus.

The cemetery was crowded, though, when they put old Alex down. Someone said they hadn't seen so many black coats and string-ties since the day after it was announced that President Lincoln had been shot in the back of the head at Ford's Theatre back in Washington, so at least folks remember, and turned out to pay their final respects in respectable numbers.

They also chipped in to buy old Alex a tall gravestone, shaped like a big, squared-off pinnacle, broad at the base and tapering upwards to the sharpened point at the top.

Ferdinand Reilly, the liveryman, who was very good at engraving on stone, chiselled in old Alex's name and pertinent data facing the roadway, and farther east, the centre of town itself.

Old Alex had been a scout, a trapper and trader, a cowman, horseman, and back during the war, a Union soldier, so a lot of people had crossed paths with him. Also, he was a big, scarred, gruff, friendly and generous man, liked by miners and cattlemen and merchants, so he had certainly not shuffled off friendless, but when the preparations to put him down were being discussed, no one could recall ever once hearing old Alex mention a church. Even Wilma Pierce Billings, his daughter and only child — in fact his only survivor — could not shed a glimmer of light on this aspect of her father's sentiments. She told her husband, Will, that as far as she could remember, they had usually been out at the ranch, come Sunday, or else, after they had moved into town, had sold the ranch and cattle and her father had got interested in civic matters, he was so busy with other things that when Sunday rolled around, he simply never quite made it to church.

She had gone, usually with friends, other budding young girls whose parents, properly gussied up, accompanied Wilma and her friend, but Alex, as far as she knew, had not been inside either one of Sioux Falls'

11

two churches in all his lifetime, and she did not recall him ever expounding about religion, and *that* made the matter of selecting a parson to speak at graveside, a little awkward.

Will resolved it. He asked *both* preachers to speak, which they did, and as a result of this, old Alex, even in death, inaugurated a fresh breakthrough for his town. Subsequently, when some cowboy or miner or other variety of little-known transient was found dead and brought to the cemetery to be put down, it became customary for both the parson and the Catholic priest to stand up and pray for the soul of the late departed.

The fee was three dollars. They split it between them.

Alex Pierce faded quickly. Three good early springs, wet and with no late frosts, had made the ranges push up feed as never before. The cowmen made money, which in turn assured the prosperity of the merchants, and throughout the Sioux Falls' countryside, there was plenty of everything, which meant that people were more congenial and tolerant, and also more forgetful of the dead.

Tolerant of everything except that trickle of emigrants the railroad people were trying to coax into riding the cars to rails-end in Dakota Territory, where they could take up land and homestead. The railroads owned every other section, so, along with the fare they collected, there was also a fair possibility that they could also sell some of that worthless land out there where, the posters back in St Louis and Chicago still said, buffalo and antelope ran in the thousands — something which hadn't been true for twenty-five years.

But, generally, those squatters did not last more than one bad winter. Still, the cattlemen resented them; they also disapproved of the railroads' promotional schemes. More than one great smoking locomotive suddenly jumped the track on its way through cattle country, and ploughed up the prairie for a hundred yards after hitting a series of emplaced iron bars on its tracks.

Some of those gunguards old Alex had first enticed to the Territory began appearing, again, in the country around Sioux Falls, but now in the employ of the railroads.

Charles Monmouth, who succeeded old Pierce as Director of the Board for the bank, was always bland when anyone mentioned the possibility of a head-on collision between railroaders and cowmen.

'Any developing area has its frictions,' he

was in the habit of saying. 'Since I've been out here I suppose I've seen maybe fifteen or twenty crises come and go. This one will do the same . . . As for the squatters . . . Well, of course the bank's shareholders and depositors are townsmen and stockmen. So far, we do not have a single squatter account. On that basis, then, I would be inclined to sympathize with the stockmen, wouldn't I?'

Ferdinand Reilly told Town Constable Jack Moses that Charley Monmouth was like a lizard, he could change his shape as well as his colours quicker than a body could say Scat.

Jack laughed. 'He's a banker, ain't he? They're different from criminals, Ferd, but in one way they ain't *altogether* different; they know which side of their cornpone the butter's on. Charley was Alex's monkey-on-a-string for six, seven years. It's habit with him by now to straddle fences. Anyway, what he said was true; homesteaders are one thing we just simply do not need out here, cluttering up the land with abandoned shacks and broken fences and such-like. This town stays healthy because the cattlemen are doing right well. Charley was right; we don't need those lousy homesteaders, but we *do* need prosperous cow outfits.'

Charley was probably right in the original context of his statement; there would not be real, serious trouble between cattlemen and railroaders. Both sides were vested, both sides were too vulnerable, and neither side was captained by men who grabbed up guns in a surge of unstable emotion and rushed forth to start shooting; at least neither side would do that on the spur of the moment, and the longer a simmering feud between hard and calculating men simmered, the less probability there was of any of them, from one side or the other, spending good money in a bad cause. Neither railroads nor cattle associations made a red cent fighting, and with the land growing, with money to be made by the wagonload in a dozen different ways, either by transporting people, feed, or cattle, by the one side, or by feeding railroad crews, passengers, and other railroad people such as the telegraphers stationed in the towns, by the other side, people might make threats and growl imprecations, but there was no real ideological difference at stake, and more to the point, they were all far more interested in making money than in fighting one another.

As Charles Monmouth had suggested, the probability of serious trouble coming between stockmen and railroaders got farther away with each passing day.

He was also right in another way; there was always some kind of trouble. Dakota Territory was growing, it was rough, largely lawless, boisterous, and was coming into its own. There were all kinds of people in the towns and out upon the ranges. Gunfights and lynchings were commonplace. Factionalism thrived; to be in the Territory during those fledgling days was to be alive in a period of constant turmoil, constant friction.

Chapter Two

MR JOHNSON

Dakota Territory was largely plains country. Someday, so the knowledgeable squatters said, the entire plain would be burnished gold with wheat and oat tops. Right now, though, it was scourged by wind, wrinkled by rain, frozen by winter and sunblasted by summer, and its immensity of briefly-blessed prairie lay golden-soft and rich-honed by the last wind of springtime, immune to all of nature's violence and turned inward to the sweet sounds of new growth stirring within itself. The prairie greened up, the creeks tamed down, the trees stirred, budding afresh, and overhead a sky the colour of robins' eggs, flecked with fat, small clouds, turned the winterlong nightmare into the warm and beautiful renewal that squatter-men felt, dumb-brute-like, to be The Promise. No one died, life was everlasting — it just slept through the winters of its soul; nature came afresh each late springtime to mutely attest, with her perennial, enduring promise, that life passed through all its phases, and was always renewed. That was The Promise.

On Sundays the squatters hitched up and drove to someone's house for their prayer meeting. They were too far from Sioux Falls to make it in, and back again, in one day, but even if they'd been able to do that, they wouldn't have; Sioux Falls was a stockman's town. A fool-hoe-man could feel the antagonism there, could sense the dangerous hostility. All a squatter had to do was drive up in his battered wagon with its thin, rough-coated team on the tongue, and climb down wearing his coarse, flat-heeled cowhide boots and his homespun shirt and britches. That was all he had to do to see the animosity in the bronzed faces of rangemen, to see the contempt in the eyes of the merchants, to feel the very air he breathed turning tainted against him.

The railroads had used them, the cowmen despised them, the land merchants had fleeced them, but every Sunday in the midst of all their hardship and demoralizing poverty, they drove to someone's homestead and had services.

Spring was past, the ploughed ground had been turned up in ropey spirals and lay fallow now, awaiting the next function in the arduous sequence which culminated

18

only when the land was sifted down, flour-fine, to accept the seed.

Early summer was on the land. It was fragrant and warm again, the womenfolk scrubbed stove-smoke residue from the walls and ceilings, dosed their young with sulphur and molasses, aired the ticking and, when the moon was right, made lye-soap and gathered herbs. On Sunday they raised worn, drab faces and Gave Thanks. They were tougher than the men — or dumber. The men Gave Thanks too, but in their secret hearts they mocked and railed at the destitution they were being thankful for receiving.

They returned to their homes in mid-afternoon, unhitched, put out the animals, changed back to their patched clothing, and grimly read from The Book by guttering coal-oil lamplight until bedtime, and thus they prepared themselves for the disappointments and the exasperations of the week to come.

Nothing varied the routine except the weather. In winter they ate less, coughed more, and prayed less for Eternal Salvation and more for the stingy store of hay in the loft to last until new grass came, otherwise their horses and milk cow would starve to death.

A man could *feel* the grinding hardship. In their shacks he could *smell* the destitution, the inescapable demoralization.

From a long way off he could see the poverty. It was like riding up a roll of land and halting at the top to gaze down upon an eternity of grassland cursed with the scattered far homesteads of aliens who had no idea at all how people in this far place should exist.

He sat up there, bearded, armed with his beltgun, his booted carbine, the Missouri-blade in its sewn scabbard inside his boot-top, chewed his cud of tobacco, and gazed at the nearest shack and soddy-barn, understanding in his one long glance exactly how poor those people had to be, down there.

He rode a powerful brown horse, a battered A-fork saddle, had his blanketroll tied professionally behind the cantle, and wore a threadbare old dark hat whose dented crown and curled brim bore the stains of dirt, nab-sweat, and food-stains from greasy fingers.

His eyes were dark, to match his hair and beard. His features, half hidden by whiskers, were neither noticeably hard, nor soft, but seemed set in an expression of constant bemusement, a kind of pensive detachment. He was powerful in build and flat-muscled.

He wore a knee-length duster that had once been white but which now was travel- and camp-stained.

As he urged the powerful brown horse down the near side of the landswell, he had no idea it was Sunday nor that those people yonder had only an hour earlier returned from The Services. He rarely knew what day of the week it was, and ordinarily he did not care a damn.

They saw him coming. The two children, a small boy and a smaller girl, fled to the house like flushed quail. The drab, flat woman gathered her apron close and shooed the youngsters inside, then she hovered in the doorway. The man, gaunt and rawboned in his baggy trousers and his high-topped cowhide boots into which his trousers had been stuffed, stood beside the tie-rack in front of the soddy-barn, watching too. The man feared rangeriders. They had never molested him, but he'd known those whom they had bedevilled. The curse of having to live apart and alone, one family to a claim, was that a man was never free of dread when he saw even a solitary rider coming.

Except that this one did not look like a cowboy. He carried no lariat, for one thing, for another thing he wore a linen duster, like a traveller. Finally, as the horseman walked his seal-brown big stout horse up close enough, and smiled through his beard, he seemed friendly.

The squatter swallowed hard, then bobbed his head. 'Light down,' he said to the dark-eyed stranger. 'Light down, brother, and if you haven't eaten we'll feed you with God's blessin', this being Sunday and all.'

The stranger leaned both hands atop his saddlehorn gazing at the squatter, chewing slowly on his cud, then he spat aside, swung off with strong grace, and said, 'Right obliged, friend, right obliged. My name is Johnson. I'm just passin' through. Mind if I put the horse up?'

The squatter minded; he had very little hay left. 'Come along,' he said, leading the way into the mouldy-smelling sod-log barn. 'My name is Joshua Barnard. I'm from Ohio, back in the States.'

As the bearded man off-saddled, then turned his horse into a stall, he wordlessly fished deep and brought forth a silver cartwheel. 'Mr Barnard, I ain't a man that drops in unexpected on folks expecting anything I don't pay for. This here is for some feed for my animal.' He pushed the big coin into the squatter's work-stiffened hand. 'And Mr

Barnard, I ain't a man that likes argument.'
He smiled through his beard, showing powerful, white teeth. He left the squatter gazing at the big coin, took up a mended pitchfork, stepped to the loft, pitched down meadow hay for the horse, came back down and shook chaff from the long duster, then went to unbuckle the saddleboot with its carbine, remove it from the saddle and hold it cradled as he said, 'I know how it is with a man, Mr Barnard. Hospitality ain't for sale. You got a Christian heart, and I appreciate that. But I know how it goes with folks trying to set up out here.'

For the squatter, that silver dollar was more than a week's wages. He was torn between handing it back and not handing it back. The burly, bearded man, with his friendly, watchful dark eyes seemed able to read him deep down. Joshua Barnard sighed, slowly pocketed the coin, got red in the face with the guilt of what he had just done, and had to admit his hardship by saying, 'If you been in my boots, Mr Johnson, you'll know how it goes when a man's got to take money for what's his Christian duty to do for his fellowmen without charge.'

Johnson's steady dark gaze did not waver. 'I been in your boots, Mr Barnard. It ain't an easy land. In fact, it ain't an easy life. Them as has it gets more, and them as don't have it gets kids. Nightfall in the towns, men with silver in their pockets set in the saloons playin' cards and drinking expensive whisky. Squatters, well, come nightfall, Mr Barnard, they got no money to take to town; whatever they do, it can't cost 'em anything. So they go to bed to save lamp-oil, and the Good Lord give 'em their woman . . . Tell me, Mr Barnard, how far are we from Sioux Falls?'

'Seven miles as the crow flies. Eight and a half miles if a body stays to the ruts. You bound for there?'

Johnson's pleasant smile came again. 'Not exactly. I been on the trail a long while. I know *about* where I am, and I know where I'm goin', you see; it's just the country in-between I ain't too sure about.'

Johnson laughed, which gave Joshua Barnard an excuse to do the same; laughter was the rarest of all things on a Dakota Territory homestead. For Barnard, it was a way to find relief for that lingering sense of guilt he had. He hadn't more than weakly smiled in a long while.

The stranger, looking like a soiled stork in his long, shapeless linen duster, continued to smile directly into Joshua Barnard's eyes

24

and, having made things easy between them, he now said, 'Like I say, it's been a long trail, Mr Barnard. My horse is tired and I'm weary myself. Now then, I'm a man of business. I don't accept no favours . . . If I could lie over here four, five days, Mr Barnard, I'd pay twenty dollars in gold.' At the odd, breathless look on the squatter's face, Johnson raised a thick hand. 'I understand, believe me I do, Mr Barnard. A man's got his Christian duty to befriend the friendless and to succour the hurt and ailing.' He dropped the hand, continued to smile, and fished inside his linen coat as he said, 'I ain't hurt nor ailing. I'm just dog-ass tired, and like I said, friend, I'm a man of business, so I don't accept no favours. I pay my way.'

He held out the dully shining twenty-dollar goldpiece. 'This here is strictly a business arrangement. You ain't beholden to me and I ain't beholden to you, which is the way things ought to be between folks, as I see it.' The dark eyes smiled. 'Take the money, Mr Barnard. I need the rest, so does my horse, and we'd both feel right obliged to you. It ain't enough, I know, but among poor folks it's better'n wages. Take it.'

Joshua Barnard took it, burning with shame and self-reproach, feeling degraded

— but rich. He had never before in his life had the opportunity to test his principles. Now he'd had that chance, standing flat-footed in his own rude soddy-barn, and Satan must have smiled because he'd sold out lock, stock, and barrel, for twenty-one dollars, part in silver, mostly in gold.

Johnson sighed, looked out into the dusty yard, looked far beyond, off in the direction of Sioux Falls, and Josh Barnard said, 'A business arrangement, then, Mr Johnson,' and pocketed the money, his head swimming with thoughts of what he needed, what Delia and the young 'uns needed, and what they could now buy. He winced when his wife's name crossed his mind. She was stronger in her conviction of the Christian way than he was; at times she was exasperatingly stubborn in her conviction. She wouldn't scold, she never did that, but she had a way of standing very erect, crossing both arms across her skinny bosom and gazing steadily at him from large, grey eyes, with her lipless, long mouth pulled back flat.

Mr Johnson was wrong about *that*, anyway, if maybe he wasn't wrong about other things. Josh Barnard didn't care for cards, but he *did* savour a drink of rye whisky now and then. As for the other —

what poor men could do at night because it was free — Mr Johnson was wrong about that.

'Well sir,' said Joshua Barnard, stirring in his tracks. 'You'll be hungry, and we'll move out the children so's you'll have a bed.'

'No,' exclaimed the bearded stranger. 'Nothing like that, Mr Barnard. I'll bed down in the loft.'

'But you paid for —'

'No; I couldn't turn out the young 'uns. Just set your mind at rest. I'll be comfortable as a tick in the loft, believe me. And from up there, a man can see all around . . . But I *could* use a meal.'

Barnard did not press this argument. If the children did not have to give up their pallet behind the stove, maybe Delia would not be so unrelenting.

They strolled up from the soddy-barn in the direction of the soddy-slab house. All around them lay the soft wonder, beauty and sweetness, of early summer.

Chapter Three

RENDEZVOUS

Southwest beyond the farthest claim where the land turned gravelly and had slate-rock scabs protruding here and there from the broken low slopes, a few trees grew, at intervals, although from a distance they looked close enough together. They were scrub trees, round and fat at the base, juniper-like, and they seldom seemed to achieve a height of more than thirty or forty feet. They did not make good stove wood because they popped unmercifully, and smoked despite the tightest stovepipe-swedgings.

In fact, they were worthless; they did not even have berries, which junipers had, so even the Indians had ignored them.

They had just one advantage; they blocked off visibility; they prevented probing eyes from seeing past or around them, and where they stood closer, forming rank-scented shade, men and horses could remain unnoticed in that speckled gloom, as long as they did not move to attract attention.

The bewhiskered man in the linen duster leaned and whittled, spat amber from time to time, looked out and around from beneath the greasy, battered wide brim of his hat, and behind him stood the powerful seal-brown horse, drowsing in the shade. They had both been there an hour, but it was still early morning, so, unless there was some reason for being impatient, they could both stand there in the shade for another couple of hours if they chose to, or perhaps even longer before they would have to move along, back towards the Barnard claim, which was something like four miles northeastward.

Two riders appeared, far southward riding inland towards the broken country where the man in the linen coat whittled. He watched their progress idly. They converged, after a while, boosted their animals over into a lope and came right on up into the broken country, right on up into Mr Johnson's shade. He closed his knife, pocketed it, tossed the whittled stick away, looked up and said, 'Morning, Abel. Morning Jasper.' The riders stepped down. They were younger men, each with a dramatic moustache, each heavily armed. They were dressed as rangemen, and their equipment as well as their clothing, boots, spurs, hats, shirts and trousers, showed a lot of wear. One, the man named Abel, was slightly gaunt and big-boned. His eyes were very pale blue, his hair was light-sandy in colour, and he moved with the easy confidence of a man who smiled or laughed a lot, and was inherently reckless. He said, 'Where'd you hole up?' to the whiskered, older man.

'At the homestead of a squatter named Barnard,' stated Johnson. 'Give him twenty-one dollars; bought him cheap. I give him the name of Johnson. You . . . ?'

Abel grinned. 'The same. I put up with a squatter name of Janicek; some kind of foreigner. Lives alone, hates the hell out of the cattle interests, don't much like the government neither, nor the President — nor the law. Sort of a mean, cranky feller, but he put me up for fifteen dollars.'

They both turned to the other man, the one named Jasper, who was grey-eyed, round-faced, with still eyes that slanted upwards slightly at their outer edges, giving Jasper a faintly Oriental look, or perhaps a faintly 'breed-Indian look. He had coarse black hair, straight as rope, and a long, wide mouth. 'I went closer,' he told Johnson and Abel. 'Went down within couple miles of Sioux Falls and put up down there with a family that's got some gawddamned goats. Their name is Holden. The lady's sickly, and they got a little girl that's puny too. The feller is broke in spirit. Damned bad, being a squatter. They've went and run off his horses a few times, and they went and shot his milk cow last autumn. I told him — your trouble is you took up land right on the edge of their damned cattle range, mister, so you'd ought to have expected what's happened to you.' Jasper shrugged thick shoulders. 'I done him a little better; I give him two goldpieces to put me up.'

Abel's pale eyes widened. 'Forty dollars?'

'It's my forty dollars, ain't it?' growled the 'breed-looking, grey-eyed man.

Abel let that slide and faced Johnson. 'We'd ought to meet in town,' he said. 'We got set up, and that was the first step. Now, we'd ought to meet in town.'

Johnson was agreeable. 'Yup. Day after tomorrow. Be just as well if we acted out bein' dog-ass tired for today and tomorrow. Keep the squatters satisfied they know all there is to know about us. Day after tomorrow maybe about high noon.'

The younger men nodded. 'Where, in town?'

'Liverybarn,' said Johnson. 'Whoever's there first just set and loaf. And be careful.'

31

Abel said, 'I'll tell you something; this old bastard I'm putting up with — Janicek — he's got it in for the cowmen, for their town, and for the feller named Monmouth who runs their bank in Sioux Falls.' At the steady look he got from the other two, Abel smiled knowingly. 'Janicek's just plain down on everyone and everything.'

Johnson wasn't interested in Janicek. 'What about the feller who runs the bank?'

'Wouldn't give a homesteader the time of day, according to Janicek. Stingy, mean and treacherous. His full name is Charles Monmouth and he come into chieftain'ship of the bank some months back when the old man who founded it died.'

Johnson spat out his cud. 'What about the *bank*.'

Abel said, 'Full to the rafters with money and placer gold, according to Janicek.'

'Oh hell,' scoffed the 'breed-looking man, Jasper. 'How would a squatter know that?'

'According to Janicek, *everyone* knows that,' retorted Abel. 'The stockmen been squirrelling it away in there since before it become a real bank. The merchants too, Janicek says he knows for a fact that a cowman named Bannion's got seven, eight thousand dollars cached away in that bank.'

Johnson leaned and eyed the pale-eyed

younger man, and said nothing as he fished forth his clasp-knife and lowered his head a little as he went thoughtfully to work paring fingernails. 'Sounds good,' he said, drolly.

Jasper agreed with that. 'Yeah, sounds good, and I sort of figure it's probably true enough. Only I remember once, three fellers dynamited a bank up in —'

'And got nothing,' broke in Johnson. 'All right. A man lives and he learns — or he don't live long, does he?'

Jasper hadn't finished. 'They got *something*.' He patted his right upper leg. 'A bullet plumb through the leg of one of 'em that killed the horse under him.'

Johnson raised calm brown eyes. 'All right. This time we'll do better. We'll make sure how much they got in their gawd-damned bank.'

'How?' challenged Jasper.

'I'll clean up, day after tomorrow, ride on in, and make a deposit with Mr Monmouth. I got two thousand in paper under my shirt.' Johnson smiled detachedly at the 'breed-looking man. 'Jasper, we don't make no mistake this time, believe me. Mr Monmouth'll tell me how safe his bank is, how much he's got in it, and how he guards depositors' money. You know, they always rub their paws when someone walks in with a new account. All right?'

Jasper was placated. 'Yeah, all right.'

Johnson kept looking at the grey-eyed man. 'Anything else, then?'

'Just the usual,' mumbled Jasper, beginning to ease off with his scepticism, in the face of Johnson's darkly calm and totally dispassionate gaze.

Johnson nodded about this. 'Well; you and I'll go in with the flour sacks like always, Jasper. Abel can mind the horses out back in the alleyway, like always too. I'll have the sawed-off twelve-gauge under my duster. Best time is about noon. Out the back door into the alleyway, and on our way. At least that's the way I figure it now, until we've ridden in and looked things over.'

Abel turned and studied his horse, which had too-long feet and needed fresh shoes. 'I'll ride in early,' he told the others, 'and get my animal shod all round.' He faced Johnson. 'Them squatters'll be able to identify us easy.'

'If they'd do it,' said Jasper. 'Where I'm put up they sure don't have no love for the constable in Sioux Falls; they say he belongs to the cattlemen.'

Johnson's comment cut right through this argument. 'They'll do it all right. You can bet money on that. The minute someone offers a reward for information, they'll fall over each other gettin' in there to give 'em descriptions.'

Jasper nodded dourly. 'I reckon. Well; it wouldn't be no secret for very long anyway, would it? They got flyers out on the Eastman gang from Miles City to Council Bluffs. Even if it wasn't us, even if it was three other fellers, the Eastman gang'd still get blamed for it.'

Johnson stooped to retrieve his whittled stick and go back to carving on it as he said, 'Tell you what I think; after this one we'd better split off and be quiet somewhere, for the rest of the year. Then, next May, we could meet in Denver again, like we done this spring.'

Abel's eyes brightened. 'Sure; at the same place too. Meet at Fanny's place. That's good for a man, setting up at Fanny's place for a few days in the springtime. It's better'n taking sulphur and molasses for thinnin' down the blood.'

Johnson grinned at Abel. 'You might be right at that.' He turned a little to face Jasper, the unsmiling man. 'Damned long ride for you,' he said, 'if you go back out to Kalispell.'

Jasper's answer was hard and practical. 'If I got a saddlebag full of money, it won't seem like no distance at all.'

'Why don't you head south?' asked Abel. 'Why d'you always want to go back up there with the In'ians and the lousy rain? That's the damndest country I ever seen, Jasper. Rains every week, towns are full of mud. Nothing to do but set around and smoke pipes and smell the In'ians.'

Jasper's grey eyes darkened a shade. 'I like it,' he replied quietly. 'You know, Abel, I ain't got light hair and light-coloured whiskers; when I go south they look at me the same as they do up here. Like I'm some sort of makeshift white man. Around Kalispell there's more In'ians and 'breeds than anything else. They don't treat me no different up there.'

Johnson heaved a big sigh, shot a squinty look at the location of the sun, pocketed his clasp knife for the second time and tossed away the whittled stick. 'I got a feeling about this one,' he said, still squinting skyward where the lowering red ball was swimming in its eternal firmament. 'We're going to see more money than we ever seen before.' He lowered his dark gaze to the pair of younger men. 'I'll head down to the Taos country and live like a king. Maybe I'll even buy that piece of land down there that Messican cow-rancher's been trying to sell me for the past four or five years.' Johnson laughed softly. 'He's got a girl named Julita who goes with the land.'

Abel nodded knowingly. 'I remember. I seen her once, when I went down there lookin' for you . . . She's pretty enough; got hair like a black bear in his prime . . . you'd have to make her shave, though. I never seen many women with them downy little black moustaches.'

Johnson's amused, detached expression lingered. 'She'd shave for her man,' he told them. 'Anyway, on a warm summer night with a full moon, you can't see her moustache.' He straightened up off the tree and said, 'We'd better head out. Day after tomorrow in the morning, out front of the liverybarn. All right?'

The younger man agreed, then the three of them went after their horses. Johnson rode out first, alone, heading in a straight line for Joshua Barnard's claim. Abel and Jasper left a little later, and split off when they were a half mile away from the rendezvous, going their separate ways.

The sun moved inexorably, but slower this time of year than it usually descended, the land lay warm and soft-blending, out where its broken segments merged with the southward flow of prairie. It was the best of all seasons to be alive, to be moving across the plain with a powerful challenge seven miles distant, with a hint of a great reward pulling a man.

Johnson fished through his saddlebags until he found a pair of dry cigars. He lit one and poked the other one back where it wouldn't be broken. The bite of the tobacco and the tang of its scent added to his secret sense of impending accomplishment. A new season lay ahead for the Eastman gang, and with luck, maybe the bank in Sioux Falls would be the only bank they'd have to clean out. *That* would be something; get enough from just one steel vault to last them all year. That would indeed be something!

Chapter Four

THE WAITING BEGINS

Delia Barnard told Joshua that there was something about Mr Johnson that she could *feel* was wrong, and Joshua, with his twenty-one dollars hidden in the bottom of the flour tin, turned placating.

'Nothing wrong that I can see, Lady.'

'Then why'd he go riding off before breakfast this morning, him a stranger to the country?'

'Well; you can't leave a big, stout animal like that seal-brown horse standin' around getting all stocked up, can you? Anyway, maybe he wants to see more of the country.'

'Yes, indeed. And for all you know he's one of those range detectives the cattlemen hire to burn out settlers — or maybe even shoot us in our bed, Joshua.'

'Listen to me,' said Joshua, in the cabin's doorway, 'we can buy a ton of grass hay from old Janicek now, and keep the cow milking until the grass is stronger. And we can get shoes for Nan and Josh Junior, with enough left over for a piece of gingham for you.' Barnard's smoky eyes softened. 'Delia; this much I've learnt out here; when an opportunity comes along, reach out and take hold of it.'

She pushed a piece of wood into the stove's firebox without looking at him, until she'd clanged closed the iron door. Then she turned, 'Joshua, there aren't any opportunities out here.'

They faced one another the width of the sooty little cobbled-together room, which was always smoky and dismal, even in the middle of summertime. He bowed a little at the shoulders. The look in her eyes was a constant reproach to him; he had *wanted* to do better by her; years back, in Ohio, he had promised to do better, too.

He said, 'Well; after summer's gone, we'll sell down to the wagon and team, if you want, and go back.' Then he stepped on through, closed the door quietly, and headed for the barn. The ploughed ground was just right now for breaking the clods with his log-and-chain drag.

Mr Johnson was off-saddling in the silence of the barn when he got down there, and that surprised him, because as a general rule he kept watch, consciously and even unconsciously, for approaching riders.

Johnson gave him a grave, dark look, then

wordlessly hoisted the saddle and rested it astraddle the harness-pole. As he turned back for the bridle he said, 'It's a big country hereabouts, Mr Barnard.'

Joshua stepped to the pole and leaned. 'Big enough for settlers as well as cowmen, Mr Johnson.'

Johnson's detached gaze showed faint irony as he drawled a response to that. 'No. No, sir, there ain't no country *that* big. I've seen it before; even where they had to ride ten miles by moonlight to chouse the cattle and horses over cliffs, and fire the haystacks and houses. There isn't *no* country big enough for them both . . . Should be, I reckon, but it never is, Mr Barnard.' Johnson took his horse to its stall, turned it in, looped the bridle from the saddlehorn and settled thoughtfully against the rough wall. 'Strange thing about folks, Mr Barnard. I seen country where you'd ride for three, four days, and never see another two-legged critter, just elk and bear and deer and such like. The only folks living out there was nomad In'ians and some cowmen. You know, that was sure-Lord big enough land for the both of 'em. Only it really wasn't; both sides would skulk round when they didn't have anything else to do, and do their damndest to wipe out the others. And by gawd, Mr Barnard, sometimes they had to ride a couple of days just to get within gunsight of one another.' Johnson showed that calm, dispassionate smile of his. 'That's how it is.'

Joshua Barnard listened, and privately agreed. 'Someday it'll be different,' he muttered. 'That's what I tell my wife; if folks just hang on and work hard . . .'

'She believe that, Mr Barnard?'

Joshua stared at his scuffed, run-over boots. 'I don't know. All she ever says is — *if* them days ever come, Joshua, you and I'll be long under the sod, so it won't do us any good, will it?'

Johnson pondered that, then fished out his tobacco plug and carved off a slice, stuck in the knife and offered both to Barnard. The squatter shook his head. 'No thanks.' He watched Johnson pouch his cud and put up the knife and plug. 'You've travelled a lot,' he said. 'Tell me where there's a good country, where the winters are not too bad, where the land is good and there's plenty of water. And where everyone don't despise settlers.'

Johnson was amused again. 'Yeah, I know such a place, Mr Barnard. Only you got to die to get up there.'

'Well; we'll be leaving in the autumn,'

stated Joshua. 'A man can buck the weather, going hungry, even being hated by his neighbours, but he can't buck the look in his woman's eyes, Mr Johnson, nor the sight of toes stickin' through the shoes on his young 'uns.'

Johnson nodded; it was an old story to him, to all rangemen. He strolled out back and saw the children at work in the warm earth creating a mud house with a mud barn. They were curly-headed and the boy, who was older, seemed small for his age. The little girl had hands that moved like pink spiders, she was quick in her movements, quick in her ability to see and do and understand. They were both happy in their ragged, patched clothes, and sure enough their toes *did* protrude. Johnson chewed, watched, and wondered what kind of a man would allow himself to be caught and held in a condition like this. They *were* dumb-brutes, as the cowmen said, they were stupid and thick-headed. All Barnard had to do . . .

Johnson turned back as Joshua led forth one of his big old horses to drape chain-harness over his back. The noise was familiar to Johnson. So was the sight. Twelve years back, a man named Roy Eastman had been burned out and whipped off, over in

Idaho, had lost everything but a Colt's dragoon revolver and a Springfield carbine. Had lost a wife and a little girl; they had left him two nights later, stealthily taking the steam cars back to Missouri. He had never seen them since, nor heard from them.

The Colt and the Springfield had enabled Roy Eastman to find his true place west of the Missouri.

Joshua Barnard led forth his other harness-horse and Johnson walked back to indifferently help him with the harness. Neither of them spoke until Joshua was ready to lead the horses out to his log-and-chain, then he smiled and said, 'I'm right obliged.'

Johnson went as far as the door and watched. The sun was good, back there, the silence was miles deep, and there was a winey scent to the air that seemed to come from far-off mountains where pine-sap was running again.

He strolled over where the children played to watch. The little girl studied him from a half averted face, eyes bright with childish interest rather than adult curiosity. He knelt, the old duster in the dirt, and without a word began selecting straight twigs from her pile, then he took some of her wet mud and began fashioning his own soddy. Both the children stopped to watch.

He worked methodically and precisely. When the boy said, 'You make a fine house,' Johnson did not look up as he replied. 'You could make one just as good; thing is, you got to work slow. You got to fit each stick and harden the sod until it'll stick just right. That way you can keep the walls from bulging out and you can keep the corners plumb. Like this.'

The little girl inched closer. She smelled of soap and wild lilac. Johnson showed her which stick to use. The little boy enviously watched, and after a while he said, 'Mister, do you always wear that long white coat?'

Johnson's calm brown gaze lifted a little. 'It helps to keep my shirt and britches clean.'

The little boy looked doubtful. 'But *it's* sure dirty, ain't it?'

Johnson accepted that. 'I reckon. Well; one of these days I'll wash it.' He stopped helping the little girl. 'What's your name?' he asked. The little boy chirped his quick answer. 'Andy. It was my maw's paw's name. Andrew. And I'm nine going on to ten, and when I'm ten I can drive the team. Mister; why don't you sleep in the house where it's warm?'

Johnson considered Andy Barnard. 'They'd ought to call you Abe.'

Both the children started upwards. Johnson smiled. 'Well, you see your first name begins with the letter A, and your second name commences with the letter B. Put them together and it comes out Abe, don't it?'

The little girl grasped this at once, and maybe Andy did too, but he did not seem to, or perhaps he didn't like the suggestion. He forgot about the dirty linen duster though, and all the other questions which had been accumulating in his mind, and that had been the man's intention; he was not going to answer any more questions, not even from a child.

Later, he strolled back to the barn, leaned on the stall of his horse and looked the animal over closely. The brown was big and powerful, deep in the chest and like steel in the legs. For a man whose occupation required flight, the brown was about as good an animal as a man could buy — or steal.

That damned Abel and his long-toed horse with its worn-out shoes. It did no good at all to try and educate Abel, but a man should always — *always*, no matter where he was or what he was doing — keep his horse well-shod and ready for immediate use. That damned Abel wouldn't reach forty. It wasn't just the way he let things slide, like the horse's feet, it was other things as well. Abel couldn't drink, and he took long chances.

Jasper was reliable, but too moody. Years back Roy Eastman had ridden with a different pair. A short, wiry, spider-fast man named Hanford, and an old hand named Bartlett. He'd lost them both in the Raton mountains near the Colorado-New Mexico line when a posse ran the three of them down in a manner no one had ever heard of before; the possemen took their horses aboard flatcars and rode the rails to within five miles of the outlaw-camp, then they jumped their damned horses off those flatcars and never drew rein again until they'd run the Eastman gang down, killed Hanford and Bartlett with their backs against a cliff, and would have killed Eastman too, if he hadn't jumped his horse off, sure to be killed, but the horse, in breaking to pieces in the canyon, had been just enough to keep Eastman from being killed too.

Some men bore charmed lives.

Johnson looked out where Barnard was breaking clods, looked over where the children were busy with their new mud structure, then sauntered to his bedroll, untied it, removed the two halves of the twelve-gauge, locked them together, examined the gun all over, slipped two big cartridges into the barrels, and carefully wiped the gun with the hem of his linen coat, then he just as carefully dismantled the gun and rolled it back into his blankets again.

He knew the Winchester was loaded and ready, like the black-handled Colt he wore under the duster. A man had plenty of time to keep his weapons in perfect shape, when he only worked maybe one or two days out of about every two or three months.

He fished deep into his saddlebags for that other cigar, lit it, shed his duster, draping it across the saddle, and walked out front to thumb back his ragged hat and stand in warm sunlight looking southeast-ward, which was in the direction of the bank in Sioux Falls.

It was not settler country, he told himself, relaxing in the warmth and glancing else-where, closer in and on all sides. A man could walk behind a team all his damned miserable life and he'd *still* never make it anything that the cowmen couldn't use better.

Barnard would be a good man to ride with — except that he wouldn't ride with the Eastman gang. He could get money, com-fort, good horses, see a lot of country, never have to grub nor sweat again. But he'd never do it, and that was too gawddamned bad because the right kind were getting harder and harder to find. The best outlaw was a mature man; the worst outlaw was younger.

Out back the little girl shrieked, her brother laughed, then he fled as she arose angrily to hurl mud after him; he had smashed her sod house.

Johnson removed his cigar, said, 'Get used to it, little girl,' then plugged the stogie back into place and forgot about the children.

Chapter Five

THE VISIT TO SIOUX FALLS

Abel's horse was fresh-shod and drowsing in a livery-barn stall by the time Jasper drifted up and without so much as a glance at Abel, out front whittling, rode right on down the liverybarn runway before dismounting. He handed the reins to a watery-eyed old hostler with orders for the horse to be rubbed down, hayed, grained, and stalled. He handed the hostler half a dollar, which was a quarter-dollar more than the charge would have been, but the only sure way for a man to know his horse would really get all the services he wanted him to have, was to pay more than was asked. Or, of course, he could stand around watching, but Jasper had no intention of doing that. He went out front into the warming early-day sunbrilliance, looked up and down the roadway without much interest, then drifted over into tree-shade where Abel was standing with one leg hooked back against the tree, whittling, and said, 'Roy ain't made it yet?'

Abel continued to whittle. 'He'll be along

. . . You see the bank up there on the east side of the road, midway?'

Jasper turned to look. 'Yeah.'

'As early as it is, there's been folks going in and coming out like bees to a honey-tree.'

Jasper's fatalistic cynicism prompted him to say, 'I hope they're *leavin'* it in there, not taking it out.'

Abel finished whittling, pocketed his knife and straightened up a little. 'There'll be plenty. Old Janicek and I got to talkin' last night. They used to hold gold bars up there, and pouches of raw gold, enough to keep a bullion coach coming and going.'

Jasper made another practical comment, his dark face turned, the smoky eyes fixed on the front of the bank. 'I'd rather have cash-money than gold bricks any day. Gold weighs too damned much.' He let his gaze drift. Several men were idly talking, over in front of a saloon, and otherwise women were trudging among the stores carrying their market baskets and wearing their sun-bonnets, and a few riders walked their horses through town.

A battered old ranch wagon with a brand burnt deeply into the wood below the driver's seat, came bouncing into town from the northeastern range, the small, hairy horses on the pole wild-eyed and ready to bolt, half broke, and green as a gourd to town noises and sights. The cowboy on the seat drove with a reckless smile; he expected a run-away and didn't give a copper coloured damn if it happened right in the centre of town.

At the forge, several patient-standing tied horses out front awaited their turn inside the shop where someone was shaping a shoe on an anvil.

Jasper saw a large man wearing the badge of a town constable cross the road and disappear into the general store. He kept watching the doorway through which the constable had disappeared as he said, 'How much law they got here, Abel?'

The pale-eyed man did not know. 'Haven't seen none yet, but it won't make no difference. We'll be gone before the law comes awake.'

A lanky, raffish man came strolling along and turned towards the barn near the shade-tree. He nodded pleasantly and said, 'Fine day, gents.'

Abel agreed with that. 'Mighty fine, friend.'

The liveryman, Ferd Reilly, walked on past and entered his little fly-specked office yonder inside the barn.

Johnson arrived a few minutes after this

brief encounter, and for a change his duster was rolled and tied behind the cantle. Except for his lack of a lariat, and one or two other small things, he might have passed for a rangeman.

He led his horse inside, solemnly overpaid the hostler to be sure the seal-brown got the best care, then he sauntered out where his friends were waiting and said, 'This here is quite a town. Bigger than expected.'

Jasper said, 'They got a town marshal; he's inside the general store. That's his jailhouse on this side of the road up yonder in the centre of town.'

Johnson nodded and rummaged the roadway until he found the bank building. Then he leaned in long silence making his study. Eventually he said, 'Abel, you looked around back yet?'

Abel had. That had been the first thing he had done after leaving his horse at the smithy. 'Yup. The alleyway runs north and south, like Main Street. It's open at both ends, only I figure, since there's some vacant land easterly behind the bank and slightly below it, we'd do better if we busted out of here in that direction. You can see some hills southwesterly, from the alleyway. We'd ought to be able to reach them in plenty of time.'

'If,' stated Jasper, 'there's no shooting, no noise to stir up the damned town.'

Johnson smiled detachedly. 'Shouldn't be no need to shoot, if we get inside and things go right.' His dark eyes moved slightly, studying the stores on both sides of the bank, studying the roadway itself, the amount of traffic, even the faces of the people who were on the plankwalks. 'Something you boys ought to have noticed by now — the safest time for a man during a robbery is right at the moment he's inside filling his flour sack. Right then folks are paralysed; they don't hardly believe their eyes; they stand around like a gang of sheep. It's afterwards when you bust out that there's danger, but inside a bank there's damned little chance of anybody doing something foolish . . . I wonder if they got any guards up there?' Johnson straightened up. 'Well, I'll see you boys directly. I got to go make a deposit up there.' He turned perfectly calm brown eyes upon the younger men, nodded and walked away.

Abel watched him cross to the far plankwalk, then he grinned and wagged his head. 'Yonder goes about the calmest feller I ever knew, Jasper.'

The 'breed also watched their leader's progress up the road towards the bank. His face was impassive and he said nothing, so it was impossible to know what he thought. Unlike Abel, whose nerves hung slack right up until he stepped into a bank and first pulled his gun, Jasper's nerves began crawling from the moment he saw Roy Eastman make his first sortie towards a bank. But Jasper's face never gave him away; outwardly, he seemed as imperturbable as a block of ice.

The morning warmed up, traffic became a little more brisk, a band of rangeriders loped into town behind a short, burly, hard-faced cowman, and that ranch wagon with the brand burnt on the side pulled away from in front of the general store, laden with a hefty load of supplies; if those little rattle-brained mustangs on the tongue tried to bolt now, they wouldn't go far, not lugging that kind of a load.

Will Billings, old Alexander Hamilton Pierce's son-in-law, was gazing out the barred front window wishing, as he commonly did on beautiful warm days, that he was still punching cows, hadn't accepted the bank job after marrying Wilma Pierce, when the dark-eyed man with the trimmed russet whiskers sidled up to his grille with a nice smile and asked to see the manager. 'My name is Johnson,' he told Will. 'I'd like to make a deposit. I'm a cattle buyer and I figure to be in these parts off and on for a few months. In fact, if business is worthwhile, I might set up here permanent.'

Will took Mr Johnson back to Charles Monmouth's desk and made the introduction. 'Mr Monmouth, this here is Mr Johnson, a cattle buyer. He'd like to open an account.'

Monmouth arose and offered a smile and his extended hand. 'Have a chair, Mr Johnson. Well sir, you chose the right place. The Merchant's and Stockman's Trust Company is as solid as the Rocky Mountains. We got assets upwards of a hundred thousand dollars — that's mostly in bonds and whatnot, but we always got ready money on hand. We got a reputation for honest dealing throughout the west . . . A cattle buyer? This here is all cattle country, Mr Johnson. We got some mighty big outfits hereabouts. If a man was looking for a place to set up permanent, he could do a lot worse than Sioux Falls.'

Mr Johnson smiled and relaxed in the chair, crossed his legs and gazed around where three cashiers, including Will Billings, were waiting on customers. 'Looks like you've got a lively bank,' he said. 'In fact, Sioux Falls seems like a right bustling community, Mr Monmouth . . . But you know, when I was ridin' in, I seen some squatter claims out a ways.'

'Oh them,' stated Charley Monmouth, with a gesture. 'They come one spring and leave the following spring. There's nothing we can do about 'em, Mr Johnson. The law gives 'em the right to take up land, and the damned railroads sell 'em passage out here. But no one worries much.'

'The cattlemen don't worry?'

'No need for them to, Mr Johnson. If the winters don't finish those squatters off, the fact that they can't raise decent crops more than one year out of three, sends them packing.' Charles Monmouth leaned on his desk and winked jovially. 'Of course, now and again, Mother Nature gets a helping hand, you understand.'

Johnson's brown eyes twinkled. 'I understand,' he said, and fished inside his shirt, drew forth his money-belt and under Monmouth's interested gaze, he drew forth and counted out two thousand crumpled notes. Monmouth hadn't expected this much and sat beaming as Mr Johnson shoved the untidy wad across the desk saying, 'I'll hold back about a thousand, Mr Monmouth. In my trade, if you got the cash on you, it sometimes makes a big difference when you're dickering with folks. You can beat a man down when you commence counting out cash-money. That's where a cattle-buyer makes his profit.'

Monmouth said, 'Of course, I understand exactly. Now if you'll excuse me I'll have Will count this again, just so's we'll both be sure, then I'll give you a receipt and set up your account.' As Charles Monmouth arose, still smiling, and walked briskly over where Billings was leaning, gazing out of the window, Mr Johnson straightened a little in the chair, studied the windows, the door-ways, one in front, one in back, and committed to memory the location of the four employees in the bank, all of them, including Monmouth, with places behind the wooden counter, out front. Lastly, Mr Johnson studied the steel safe. It was tall, taller in fact than most bank safes, being about as tall as a man. And it sat on cast-iron wheels. It was taller than it was either wide or deep, and the entire front of the thing was a steel-layered door with a combination lock and a shiny nickel-plated handle, one slightly above the other. Someone had painted a pair of sailing vessels, both with all sails billowing, scudding hull-down across the door, the big ships running in a heavy sea while above them was a wind-whipped, cloudy sky. It was a handsome decoration for a safe. Johnson liked it better than some of the paintings he'd seen on bank safes. Of course, it had nothing at all to do with the purpose of the big steel crate it was painted on, but Johnson had never seen one of those paintings that *did* have a damned thing to do with steel safes.

Charles Monmouth would have the combination. If he wouldn't open the door, there was that young buck over at the steel front wicket, the one who had first spoken to Roy Eastman. Someone always opened a safe; no one ever willingly did it, but they always *did* it. The alternative was a bullet in the body. Not even bankers like Charles Monmouth stood adamant too long when they had only one of those two choices.

Johnson saw no guards, but he noticed that all the windows were steel-barred — from the inside — and that there were a pair of those great steel doors open on both sides of the wooden doors leading into the bank from out front, and leading out of the bank by the rear exit. With that kind of protection, burglary would be almost no problem at all. Johnson smiled to himself; burglars rarely ever busted a bank. It was the men who walked in *after* those invincible steel panels had been pushed back, who robbed banks.

Charles Monmouth returned and handed some papers to Mr Johnson. He remained standing, which was Johnson's cue, so he arose, gazed at the receipt, shook Monmouth's hand and allowed himself to be personally escorted to the roadside front doorway. Will Billings nodded and smiled, too, as Mr Johnson walked past.

At the door he had to pump Monmouth's hand again, then he was out of the bank in the golden sunshine, glancing southward down where that huge old cottonwood tree stood outside the liverybarn. There were two idling men down there, gazing up in his direction.

Chapter Six

RECONNOITRING

They went up to the Drover's Rest Saloon, and in order to get there had to walk past the jailhouse, a gunsmith's shop which was next to the jailhouse, and beyond that, was the Drover's Rest.

All three of them saw the big man with the badge on his shirtfront who was talking with a short, burly cowman out front. In fact Abel nodded and smiled at Constable Moses, which annoyed Mr Johnson; this was exactly the kind of unnecessary flourish Abel was addicted to; and Johnson did not like it, had never liked it, had in fact lectured Abel about it, without one bit of success. This time, he looked coldly at Abel, who ignored the look, then they entered the saloon heading across towards the bar.

It was early in the day for saloon-trade; that did not pick up until evening, after supper, usually. Still, three dusty, corral-stained rangeriders were grouped at the upper end of the bar talking quietly back and forth, then snickering, and at a round poker table over near the sunshiny window, several older men, hatted and coated as though it were chilly, which it certainly wasn't, were unsmilingly playing cards. Otherwise, except for the fleshy, paunchy barman, who parted his black hair straight down the middle and brushed it sleekly back on both sides, the big old gamey-scented saloon was empty.

Johnson had a shotglass of rye whisky. Jasper had a beer, and Abel also had a shotglass-jolt, but he asked to have the bottle left. After the barman walked away with a crumpled greenback from Mr Johnson in his fist, Jasper said, 'Well . . . ?'

Johnson answered bluntly. 'The safe's as tall as a man, and stands directly in front of the roadside window, but across the room along the back wall. They got four people behind the counter, the manager and three clerks. I'd say that safe is chuck-full of money.' Johnson paused then offered a small smile. 'Includin' the two thousand dollars I deposited.' He downed his drink, shoved the glass away and leaned down again to resume his recitation.

'Jasper, the minute we step inside, you move to that front window and pull the blind. That way, no one can see the safe from outside. Afterwards, you go down the wickets shovin' in the flour sacks. I'll move behind the counter and throw down on 'em from behind. I didn't see weapons, not even in the corners where they usually plant a shotgun or two around banks.'

Abel said, 'Gunguards?'

'Nope,' stated Johnson, and stopped speaking when the barman returned. Johnson and Jasper shook their heads, but Abel curled a big fist round the bottle in front of him and smiled at the bartender, who walked away again. This time, Abel refilled his shotglass. The other two declined when Abel offered the bottle.

Johnson spoke again, when they were quite alone. 'Noon would be the time to bust it. Abel, you know where the back door is leading out of the building. Be there.'

Abel was agreeable. He lifted the shotglass and dropped its liquid lightning straight down. Johnson and Jasper impassively eyed the rawboned, pale-eyed man.

That blocky-built, grizzled cowman who had been conversing with Constable Jack Moses out in front of the jailhouse, walked in, saw the three cowboys at the upper bar, and went stumping off in their direction. The barman called a genial greeting.

'Morning, Mr Bannion.'

The cowman nodded, called for a bottle and a glass, and edged in among his riders. The barman went up there, smiled mechanically at something someone said, picked up the silver Bannion had tossed down, and went along to his cash drawer.

Johnson and Jasper leaned thoughtfully, feeling the euphoric warmth spreading out through their bodies, entirely content. Abel had another shot of whisky. Jasper said, 'When; tomorrow?' and Johnson inclined his head.

Abel leaned. 'Why tomorrow?' he asked quietly, argumentative now that he'd diluted the last of his normal inhibitions. 'Why not day after tomorrow, or maybe even the day after that? I sort of like what we're doing, shoving our feet under a real supper table every night, settin' in the sun and —'

'Tomorrow,' said Johnson, evenly, gazing at his bearded countenance in the backbar mirror. 'Abel, keep your gawddamned voice down. You boys ride in like you done today, only an hour or so later. I'll meet you. Abel, when you see me comin', take the horses into the alley out back, you understand? That's where I'll ride down and hand over mine. No hurry, except that it's all got to be ready, come noon. Jasper . . . ?'

'Don't fret. I'll be there.'

'Abel . . . ?'

'I know what to do, gawddammit, only I still don't see what the big rush is. This is a nice town. We could loaf a spell, couldn't we?'

Johnson finally turned his head. He did not answer, he simply stood there gazing at Abel, then he reached, caught hold of the whisky bottle and pulled it away from Abel and set it off on his left. Then he said, 'You can loaf after it's all over and you're on your way. If this here bank's got what it looks to have, believe me, Abel, we'll *all* be able to afford a few months off for loafing. But right now, gawddamn you, don't you touch another drop of liquor until after tomorrow, and don't you start another argument.'

Those rangemen from up the bar broke up, heading for the door. One of them went down where the barman was rinsing glasses in a bucket and put down some money. Then the cowboy turned, raked an indifferent glance along the faces of the three men farther along, nodded when Abel met his glance, and turned to go to catch up to his companions who had already left the saloon.

Abel stepped back. 'Jasper, you see the mean look that subbitch give me just now?'

Jasper had seen nothing. Neither had Johnson, but he had seen the cowboy on his left, so he straightened around to look. The cowboy had heard himself called a son of a bitch, and stopped mid-way to the door. 'Mister,' he called back softly to Abel, 'you wasn't by any chance talkin' about me, was you?'

Abel was already standing clear of the bar. He faced the rangeman, willing and ready. 'Mister, any time a man puts a mean look on me, take m'word for it, he's goin' to get what he's looking for.'

'Mister,' said the bronzed, whipcord cowboy, 'I didn't put no mean look on you. But you sure as hell called me a fightin' name, and *that's* somethin' don't no man walk away from.'

The barman protested to the cowboy. 'Let it go, Cal. He didn't mean nothing. Anyway, they's strangers; maybe where they come from men call one another —'

'Keep out of it,' growled the cowboy, fully facing Abel now, and, in Johnson's experienced view, probably capable of killing Abel. He looked entirely gunhandy, and that was something only other gunhandy men usually recognized.

It would be too late to find another horse-holder. Besides, a gunfight now would stir

66

up the whole town, including the constable, which meant the lawman just might want to lock Johnson and Jasper up, and he also might get to ploughing through old wanted posters, and find their likenesses.

Johnson was furious, deep down, not at the cowboy, at Abel and his asinine behaviour; he never could handle even three, four glasses of whisky. Johnson moved slightly, turning as though to protest to the cowboy, and tilted up his gunbarrel. No one noticed, until he cocked the Colt; *that* was a sound people noticed.

The cowboy discernibly stiffened. His face did not move, but his eyes did, they fell to Johnson's drawn sixgun. Afterwards they raised very slowly to Johnson's face.

Johnson was mad enough to kill someone; he was completely raging inside, but all he said to the cowboy was, 'He's been drinking, friend, and he never could handle it. Look; I apologize for him, but I ain't going to stand here and watch him get shot, either. Like I told you, I apologize for him. I'm downright plumb sorry it happened. Now then, cowboy, you turn and walk out of here, don't look back, don't touch your gun, and don't go hunt up your friends and come back. He did a plumb stupid thing. I don't mean to be tough with you, only I can't stand around watching you shoot him. Walk on out of here!'

The cowboy walked out, the doors swung back, the barman heaved a sigh that was audible all the way over where those oldsters were completely absorbed in their card game, then the barman walked down, picked up that bottle Johnson had taken away from Abel, turned and very resolutely marched off with it. The barman also knew — now — that he had one of those customers who came along now and then, who simply had no business drinking at all.

Jasper gazed stoically at Abel for a moment, then nudged him and turned towards the door. 'Let's go. You had your drink, now let's get away from here.'

The three of them moved off. Still, those oldsters up at the far end of the room next to the window, did not realize anything had happened. The barman did not tell them, either. He was in no mood to stand and answer the interminable questions those old devils would ask.

Abel was not entirely subdued, but he was quiet, as he walked between Johnson and Jasper in the direction of the liverybarn.

Johnson saw that bronzed cowboy over in front of the gunsmith's shop, talking earnestly with his friends, the other rangeriders. He prayed they would get past unnoticed. It did not quite work out that way; they were noticed, but that burly, grizzled cowman named Bannion growled when the cowboy and his cronies turned to watch Johnson and Jasper escort Abel on southward, over across the road, and that was just as well, as far as Johnson was concerned.

He was still icily furious down at the barn when the hostler brought forth their horses, then stood around being helpful in the hopes of picking up another two-bit piece. All he got was a cold nod from Johnson as the three riders did not return to the front roadway, but rode through to the back of the barn and left town in that direction, westerly.

Jasper rolled a cigarette and lit it, riding with looped reins. He did not look at either of his companions but made a solemn long study of the onward countryside.

Johnson rode like stone for a mile before he faced Abel. 'Listen to me,' he said, in a half-choked tone of voice. 'You gawddamned stupid idiot; this here is the bank we been looking for all year. All last year *and* this year . . . What the hell did you figure, back there in that saloon? You damned fool, that cowboy would have killed you. Don't give me that look, Abel. I *know* he would have. I know his kind and you aren't in their league at drawing and firing . . . In fact, Abel, I'll tell you something. You ain't worth a good gawddamn for anything at all, except horse-holding. That's not much of a job, horse-holding. By gawd you liked to not even lived through to do *that*, today. And you liked to ruin everything else for us.'

Abel blustered. 'You didn't see the fightin' look that cowboy give me, Roy. He turned and looked at me, just as plain as day, wanting to fight. I seen —'

'All he did,' stated Jasper quietly, trickling smoke, 'was put down some money for the barman, then, when he turned to leave, he give us all a casual glance because we was right there in his line of sight as he turned. Abel; I was looking at him too, and he didn't make no mean look at you or nobody else . . . Abel, you just drunk down your liquor too fast, and it come up in you bringing on the meanness. That's all there was to it, pure and simple.'

Abel flung around towards the 'breed. 'Jasper, you called me a liar. You as good as come right out and —'

'*Shut up,*' roared Johnson. 'Abel, you shut up now. You're not going to pick no fights

70

out here either. You're going to go on back to your squatter's place, eat good tonight, get plenty of sleep — don't you touch another drop of liquor — and in the morning you drift back into Sioux Falls like you're supposed to do, and mind you do exactly what you always do.'

Abel sulked, which Johnson viewed with contempt, but he did not upbraid Abel any more, and when the younger men came to the place where they would split off, Johnson said, 'See you in town tomorrow,' in his normal tone of voice, reined northwesterly, and set the seal-brown into a comfortable, mile-eating lope.

Finally, with the Barnard shack and soddy-barn in sight, Johnson confided in his horse. 'I'll kill that son of a bitch tomorrow. If he so much as opens his mouth at the wrong time tomorrow, after we're out of there, I'll kill him!'

Chapter Seven

A DAY'S SLOW ENDING

Joshua Barnard had been sod-busting for two full days and had two more full days of it ahead of him. He did not actually mind doing it, which was just as well because once the soil had been ploughed over into its ropey furrows, if a man waited a day too long the earth would be too dry and would not crumble properly, while if it was busted too early, it would be too wet, and roll up in the chains dragging behind the log. There was just one precise period for clod-busting, and when the day arrived, Joshua was out there.

He did not mind any of the work on his claim. He had never been lazy, and if it had to do with the soil, he liked doing it. Except that in Dakota Territory there was so much more than just the soil. There was the disapproval, the despair, the eventual defeat that a man saw coming towards him for a year before it arrived, and against which, no matter what he did nor how hard he worked, he was not adequate.

He was thinking of these things in the

barn near the close of the day when Mr Johnson returned from his horseback ride. Joshua nodded, not the least interested in where Mr Johnson had been, and continued at his work of hauling the harness off his team.

Johnson cared for his horse, helped Joshua put up the team, and afterwards as they leaned in the pleasant evening listening to one of the most soul-satisfying sounds a stockman ever hears — horses eating — Joshua said, 'I got to take the wagon down-country a-ways in a day or two and fetch back a jag of hay from a settler named Janicek.'

Johnson looked over with interest. 'Janicek . . . ?'

'Yes. He come out four, five years ago, and he hung on. But he's alone, and he don't need much.'

'Odd name,' murmured Johnson.

Joshua agreed with that. 'Yes, but back in Ohio, around the steel-mill towns they had lots of names like that. Folks called them people "bohunks". Mr Janicek has three claims. He bought out two families who gave up couple years ago. He farms almost a hundred acres in oat hay each year. Even some of the cowmen go to him in winter-time for horse-hay. You know what Janicek does; charges them twice as much for a ton of his oat hay, then *gives* one ton to a squatter who's out of hay.' Joshua's eyes twinkled. 'Janicek's a strange man, in some ways. He once told me the cowmen remind him of the horsemen where he came from in Europe — they ride around with whips and guns harming folks. He's a man who knows how to hate, I'll tell you that; he's a foreigner, and they make fun of him for that too, in Sioux Falls. But he had a lot of hate in him even before he homesteaded.'

Johnson thought of Abel riding in at the Janicek claim today, sullen and a little drunk. He said, 'Mr Barnard, is this Janicek a church-going man?'

Joshua sadly shook his head. 'He don't go to meetings, Mr Johnson. Some of the folks have tried to get him to, but he won't go.'

'Does he drink?'

'A little. I've smelt it on him now and then, but I've never seen him drunk.'

Johnson sighed to himself. Abel would make out all right, then . . . The damned idiot.

Joshua fingered some cracked leather on a harness-britching and pretended to be concerned about it as he spoke again. 'You figuring on staying over after tomorrow?' he asked, without looking at Mr Johnson.

It had never taken very much perception to see that Joshua Barnard's woman — whom he always referred to as 'Lady' — resented having Mr Johnson on the claim. The dislike was mutual, although Mr Johnson never showed like or dislike for people. He knew why Joshua had asked that question.

'No,' he replied. 'I'll be leaving first thing in the morning, Mr Barnard. I'm right obliged to you folks for putting me up. About that load of hay; my horse's just about eaten up all you had in the loft.' Johnson fished forth a gold coin and held it out. 'Hay's right dear this time of year, Mr Barnard. Take it.'

Joshua turned, saw the ten-dollar goldpiece, and slowly raised his eyes. 'I'll take it, Mr Johnson, but I'd as leave put my hand into a corn-chopper.' He accepted the coin. 'If I ever get out of this condition, I'll never get into it again.' He pushed the coin deep into a trouser pocket. 'I'm beholden to you and I won't forget it.'

Johnson was not embarrassed by this, but he did not particularly like it either, so he turned to his saddle on the pole and removed the linen duster from behind his cantle, shook it out and lay it across the saddle. He would have to wear the duster tomorrow, otherwise he could not enter the bank carrying the sawed-off shotgun. A man could conceal a full-sized rifle beneath his duster, if he was of a mind to. He said, speaking in a deliberately casual tone, 'I rode into Sioux Falls today. That's more of a town than I expected. Busy as a kitten in a box of shavings.'

Joshua rallied. The change in viewpoint was acceptable to him. 'It's a good town,' he conceded. 'Of course, it's a cowman's town, but still and all, excepting they don't have a doctor down there, you can get just about anything else in Sioux Falls.'

Johnson continued to stand half turned away over by the saddle pole as he said, 'I saw a husky feller wearing a badge on his shirtfront. I reckon he'd be the marshal.'

Joshua nodded. 'Jack Moses,' he stated. 'Town constable. The cowmen own him.'

'He the only lawman down there?'

'Yes. They have a vigilance committee that's made up of some of the merchants; six or eight in number. Sometimes, when Mr Moses needs a posse, those fellers ride with him. But Sioux Falls don't have much trouble. It's not like it was a trail-town nor a border-town. The big cow outfits don't tolerate trouble from their riders in the town.' Joshua's lips curled downward. 'On

76

the range, or in squatter-country, the cow outfits don't check-rein their men. Only in town.'

'Southwest of Sioux Falls,' said Johnson, 'there's a roll of hills far off. You can see them from the back alley on the east side. Any settlements over in there?'

'No. That's called the badlands; it's full of pot-holes and rock and lava beds. Even the cowmen got no use for that country, Mr Johnson.' Joshua looked over. 'If you was figuring on riding off in that direction, you'd do better to take the stageroad southward, on down where it cuts out and around the badlands. There's feed down that way, and plenty of places to camp. There'd be no point to going through the badlands.'

'If a man stayed on the stageroad, would he find another town, Mr Barnard?'

'Fargo,' replied Joshua. 'But it's a long way off. You'd be several days crossing the prairie before you saw it. It's another cowtown. They had some serious trouble down near there a few years back when a trainload of German emigrants showed up down there to claim land . . . They called out the army to put a stop to it.' Joshua lifted a work-stiffened hand to the cracked leather of the harness and felt for serious breaks. There were none — yet — but before the

77

season was out that entire set of harness would be worn out.

The sun was lowering, shadows stood along the east side of the barn, and up yonder, on the east side of the house too. Smoke drifted straight into the still late-day air from the stovepipe above the house, a stingy little tendril of it because Delia had to use her cooking-wood sparingly. They had to go miles northward to find trees worth cutting, and that took Joshua away from his farming. Nothing came easy.

After a while Joshua went up towards the house, out back of it actually, where the wash-stand was, to scrub up before supper, leaving Mr Johnson alone in the barn. He carved a sliver off his plug, pouched it into his cheek and sat down upon a small keg staring out back across the still and quiet prairie, thinking back to another place, another time, another squatter with a family.

She had never written, which was probably just as well. Or maybe she had, and over in Idaho the letter had been lying, gathering dust.

He knew where she had gone because that was where he had courted her; back to her parents' farm in Missouri. Maybe, after tomorrow and with nothing pressing for a few months, he would go back there. He'd had this thought before, and it had always ended up the same way.

No, he wouldn't go back. The notorious Eastman gang would be known of even that far away. Missouri was a place where outlaws, especially after the Civil War, had not been viewed the same way folks considered them elsewhere. The Youngers and the James' boys were heroes in Missouri. But Cole was in a penitentiary, Jesse James was dead, his brother, so Roy Eastman had heard, was somewhere out in California. Times had changed; the old heroes might not be so heroic any more. But one way or another, when a man had a price on his head, he was a fool to take chances. All the same, maybe someday he'd go back and see them. His daughter — hell — she wouldn't know him anyway.

A slight movement in the doorless front opening of the barn made him swing half around. The little girl was standing there, wearing a flour-sack apron like her mother's apron, and with both hands clasped behind her back staring curiously in at him.

He said, 'Well now, missy, you get that sod house built like I showed you?'

Thus encouraged, she entered the barn and halted nearby. 'My brother broke it,' she replied, her blue eyes round with indignation. 'He's always breaking things. Maw says he'll grow to manhood hating, and the Good Book's against that.'

Johnson pursed his lips. This was the longest speech she'd said in front of him. Usually, she eyed him askance and remained a respectful distance away. She was small and he was large. Also, she did not see many bearded men, not men who went everywhere with a shellbelt and holstered Colt around their middle.

'Maw says to tell you supper'll be ready directly.'

He returned her level, grave stare, and nodded. 'I'm obliged you come to tell me. Your name is Nan?'

'Yes. My brother's name is Joshua Andrew after my paw and grandpaw.'

'A good name,' he told her. 'Comes from the Bible. Seems to me Joshua was a soldier . . . Well, anyway, you got a nice name too. I once knew a little girl named Constance. That was her maw's name too. I knew her when she was about your age, maybe six or seven.'

'I'm seven. Where did you know her?'

'Well; over in Idaho.'

'Did she die?'

He blinked. 'Die? No, she didn't die. What made you figure that?'

'You said you *knew* her, and that made it sound like you don't know her no more.'

'Oh. Well; she moved away.' Johnson cleared his throat. 'Your maw's a good cook,' he said, gently bringing things around to safer ground.

The bright blue eyes continued their grave examination of the man. 'When you go away in a day or two, mister, are you going to see that other little girl again?'

Johnson's dark eyes remained on the child throughout an interval of thoughtful silence before he said, 'Maybe, someday.' Then he slapped his legs and arose. 'I reckon we'd best hike back to the house. I got to wash up before supper.'

She had to tilt her head far back to look up into his face. 'Don't you never take that gun off?'

He laughed and offered a thick hand. 'You ask more questions than a fortune-teller, Nan. Come along now, or your maw'll be sending down your brother to see if the wolves got us.'

They walked out of the barn into the last red rays of the dying day, and paced along in the direction of the house. The man had to take uncomfortably small steps because the child clung to his fingers, holding him back. Her hand was damp but the grip was surprisingly strong. He wondered what would become of her in the years to come.

One thing he was sure of, whatever became of her wouldn't be easy. Nothing much was easy in this life — unless it was finding a bank like that one in Sioux Falls, and that was more of a windfall than anything else. No one had that kind of luck more than maybe two or three times in all his lifetime.

Chapter Eight

MAKING CERTAIN

According to Mr Johnson's calculations there was no need to hurry, so he rode slowly, savouring the pleasant warmth of the newday morning. He was wearing the duster, so he looked the same as he departed from the Barnard claim as he had looked when he had first appeared, back there.

Otherwise, though, he was plumb rested, his seal-brown horse was full of power and endurance under him, and the hardest part was over; he was on the move, the waiting, reconnoitring, backing and filling, was over. That poor damned numbskull back there with his sod barn and his juiceless, waspish woman, would never again enter the life of Roy Eastman; the hardest part was finished, the best part lay directly ahead, down where sunlight spanked windowlights, and an occasional metal roof as well.

It took a little while to ride seven miles. He was the farthest from Sioux Falls of the three of them, which meant the other two would be in town perhaps as much as an hour before he could arrive there.

There was no point in loafing around Sioux Falls for a couple of hours before hitting the bank. Anything could happen when three men were idling away time. Mr Johnson already knew how long it took to reach Sioux Falls from the Barnard claim; he coupled this knowledge with his conviction that it would be better if he did not arrive in town until shortly before high noon, and he rode accordingly.

An hour before he touched the north roadway and pushed southward along it, he had seen the dust rising; Sioux Falls was a bustling place, for a fact.

Closer, he saw the pedestrian and roadway traffic, and confided in the seal-brown it would sure simplify things a heap if most of those folks would go somewhere and set down to eat, come noon.

He rode down into town, reined clear to avoid some loping rangemen, saw the pair of indolent men in tree-shade out front of the liverybarn, and made his way directly down there. As before, he nodded, but that was all, then entered the barn, but instead of handing over his horse to the hostler, he flipped him a two-bit coin, said, 'Maybe later,' and led the horse out to the tree where Abel and Jasper stood.

'Thought you was going to be in the alleyway,' he said to Abel, and Jasper answered shortly. 'He can't. There's a gawddamned freight wagon blockin' the alley, Roy. They've been off-loading its cargo to the general store.' Jasper's grey gaze was flat and shades darker than usual. 'Be another hour at the least before they move that gawddamned rig down out of there. We figured it'd only look suspicious if Abel went up there and led the horses. We waited over here for you.'

Roy Eastman looked up the busy roadway, looked out where the fragrant summertime day was gold-flecked with pure sunshine, and wagged his head. He had been positive when he'd left the Barnard place, just from the 'feel' of the day, that everything was going to go off clean as clock-work, today.

Abel said, 'An hour ain't too long, Roy.'

That was true; it was still early enough so that if the freight wagon was another hour blocking the back-alley, it wouldn't pitch a clod into the churn. But the question was: Would the damned wagon be out of the alley within an hour?

He growled back at Abel. 'An hour ain't too long, so long as it don't stretch into *two* hours, Abel.'

'It won't,' stated Jasper. 'The old man who clerks in the store told me it wouldn't take more'n an hour, and they been out there now for half that length of time.'

They stood in tree-shade eyeing the people, the rigs, the saddle animals, that constantly came and went. Sioux Falls was indeed a thriving place.

Constable Jack Moses ambled by and nodded, on his way into the barn for his saddle animal, and Abel smiled broadly about that, without commenting; it certainly would work no hardship on the Eastman gang if the lawman was out of town when they busted the bank.

Ferd Reilly, the liveryman, came ambling out, chewing a straw, his stomach being supported from below by a wide garrison belt. He was not exactly a *fat* man; in fact everywhere but out front Ferd Reilly was thin, his legs and arms were scrawny, his shoulders were pointy and narrow, his face was long and angular. Only out front did his body appear mis-shapen. He had a paunch about the size of a big watermelon.

Reilly was a shrewd man. He smiled easily and often, and sometimes the smile never left Ferd Reilly's face for hours on end. It was his mask. Roy Eastman read Reilly like an opened book the moment the liveryman ambled up into tree-shade and started talking; Ferd Reilly had seen these three men before, and had perhaps wondered about them — who they were, what they were doing in Sioux Falls, why they didn't stable their horses today. It was more or less natural; in every town there was at least one nosey individual. It was more or less natural that it'd be the liveryman.

Ferd used the customary openers by saying, 'You boys are sure well-mounted. Them is a fine trio of horses. You can figure that's a compliment, comin' from me. I been in the horse business most of my growed life. I know good stock when I see it.'

Abel gazed disinterestedly at Ferd Reilly. Jasper only glanced, once, then put his full attention upon Roy, who said, 'They aren't for sale, liveryman, if that's what you've got in mind. Hard enough to find good horses, without selling them.'

'Sure,' agreed Ferd, smiling widely at Roy Eastman. 'Well; you can't cuss a man for tryin'. By the way, if you fellers would like to stall your animals through the heat of the day, later on, I got plenty of extra stalls. No charge; you been good customers the past few days. No charge today.'

Roy Eastman's detached, bizarre smile

lingered on the liveryman without any of the three waiting men saying a word. They stood there and stared, and said nothing. Ferd nodded all around, raised a hand in a small gesture, a sort of departing salute, then he turned and ambled back into the liverybarn.

Abel sighed. 'Nosey old bastard.' He forgot Ferd Reilly. 'Take my reins,' he said to Jasper. 'I'll amble over and see if that damned freighter's fixing to pull out yet.'

As Abel strolled across the roadway, his companions soberly eyeing his progress, Jasper said, 'He's all right. He was embarrassed this morning, about what he done yesterday. He's all right as long as he's off liquor.'

Roy Eastman said nothing.

Abel returned in fifteen minutes, and winked at his partners. 'All right; they're pulling out southward. Give 'em ten minutes and the rig'll be clear of the alley.'

Eastman looked at the sun, looked up the roadway where there seemed to be less traffic, and, reins in hand, turned to mount his horse as he said, 'All right. Abel, take Jasper's horse and yours, head across and up the alleyway. I'll make my look-out-sashay, and meet you back there in a few minutes.'

Jasper stood alone when the others departed, but not for long. His role was in some ways the simplest role of all. He turned up the plankwalk, ambled up as far as the jailhouse, crossed to the opposite side of the road and paused out front of the general store to roll a smoke — and to critically scan the faces of everyone in his view from this spot forward, up in front of the bank. There was no lawman up there, and not even any armed rangeriders. There were some townsmen moving back and forth, in and out, but they were not near the bank, they were across the road from it, or were southward a door or two.

The front way, as far as Jasper was concerned, was accessible and wide open. He dropped the match, inhaled smoke, started forward again, and exhaled smoke.

Jasper made the second-to-last judgement, and he was satisfied as he continued his stroll. The last and final judgement was made by Eastman himself. Just before entering the bank, he would pause and make a study of everything out front, up and down the roadway, and he would then step through into the bank, and make certain everything in there was also satisfactory. Then he would pull the twelve-gauge from beneath his linen duster, which would be Jasper's cue to also step inside and draw a gun.

It had been said that the James-Younger gang had had the best organization for robbing banks, but Roy Eastman had never agreed with this; any time there were six, eight, or ten men involved, they were going to get in each other's way.

He rode slowly around through the town looking for anything suspicious. If someone had discovered who they were, somehow, and the town had secretly organized an ambush, it wouldn't be the first time an outlaw band had been caught on foot and shot down to the last man.

But there was nothing; people paid no attention to Roy Eastman on his big handsome seal-brown horse. He completed the circuit and drifted over to the east side of the main thoroughfare, reached the alleyway and turned southward down it.

Abel was standing easy, rolling a smoke, the reins to his and Jasper's horse draped over one arm. He hardly more than glanced up when Roy Eastman appeared, then finished making the smoke, popped it between his lips, lit up from a match fired up off the seat of his britches, and accepted the seal-brown's reins.

'Plumb normal,' he said to Eastman. 'Most dangerous thing I seen was a black bitch with four little puppies. She took 'em through a hole in that fence yonder.'

Eastman did not speak. He stepped to the rear of his saddle, untied the blanketroll back there, pulled out the two halves of his scattergun, retied the bedroll and calmly stood in the sunlight of the empty alleyway putting the twelve-gauge together. When that job was done, he opened the front of his linen coat, hooked the shotgun to his gunbelt on the left side, muzzles down, then closed the coat and straightened up, gazing at Abel.

'Ten minutes,' he said, and stepped past, heading for the narrow little smelly passage between two buildings which would take him back to Main Street.

Abel stood, smoked, waited, and listened. If he heard gunshots round front he immediately put the reins over the heads of their horses and waited in the saddle. If he did *not* hear gunshots, he still put the reins over the heads, but he continued to stand there on foot, just in case, when his partners arrived in a rush, they needed ground-help, either mounting or handling the loot.

He had the easiest and safest job of them all.

In front of the bank, but across the road, Jasper had bought a handful of cigars for

Eastman and a sack of makings for himself.

He saw Eastman step up on to the yonder plank-walk from between those two buildings south of the bank, saw three rangeriders jog northward side by side, talking and paying practically no heed to anything around them as they passed across Jasper's line of vision, temporarily obliterating Roy Eastman. Otherwise, Jasper was ready to proceed, so he stepped down into the dust and hiked on over where Eastman had come to a halt a few yards south of the bank's front doorway. As they came abreast Jasper held out the fistful of stogies.

Eastman's dark eyes brightened slightly as he accepted. He pocketed all but one, and ducked his head to light that one. As he did this he mumbled a question. 'How does it look to you, Jasper?'

'Looks all right; seems like the traffic's slacked off the last hour, and by my count can't be more'n three customers inside now.'

'Was there more?'

'Yeah; been quite a slug of folks go into that bank, then come back out again, directly.'

Eastman, savouring the cigar, smiled. 'That sure helps us folks in the banking business — depositors. Your gun ready?'

Jasper nodded, and watched Eastman step past, strolling methodically, and turn in at the bank doorway. Jasper dropped the right hand to his Colt, stepped to the same doorway but remained outside watching the roadway for a moment or two longer. He did not move until he heard Eastman speak inside, then Jasper stepped through, reached for the door to close it, stepped around behind Roy, whose cocked shotgun was up and swinging, to pull down the roadway blind. Jasper did not really look, not right then because he had other things to do which were critically important, but he saw from the edge of his eye that none of the people on either side of the counter were moving. They all stood like statues.

Chapter Nine

THE RAID

All three customers out front of the tellers' wickets were women. Behind the polished wooden counter Charles Monmouth had arisen from his desk when Roy Eastman entered the bank. Monmouth was still wearing half that welcoming smile he'd dredged up as he'd seen the big-depositor named Johnson step in from the roadway.

Will Billings had both hands on top of the counter. He had been counting out silver for a woman customer. Will had a gun under his counter on a shelf, and Will was a good man with a gun, but this time he was caught completely unprepared. Even if he'd had an opportunity to reach down under there unobserved by the pair of gun-wielding bank robbers by the doorway, he'd have been too completely astonished to do it.

The other two clerks, one of whom was actually a bookkeeper, were standing in conversation near the high table which was to one side of the steel safe, used by the

94

bookkeeper. They, like Monmouth and Billings, were stunned into immobility at the sight of that big-bore scattergun in the hands of the dark-eyed, bearded man with the crumpled old hat, wearing a linen duster which was none too clean.

Bank robberies were not all that rare, but they certainly were in Sioux Falls. The Merchant's & Stockman's Trust Company had been in business a quarter of a century and there had never before been so much as a rumour that it might be robbed. Back in old Alex Pierce's day no band of outlaws in their right mind would have made the attempt; old Alex had kept some of the best gun-fighters in the Territory on the company's payroll.

There hadn't been an armed guard inside the building in ten years, now.

Eastman told Billings and Monmouth to get over by the safe. They obeyed without any hesitation. He told the oldest of the pair of men near the high table to stand apart, and when they also obeyed, he pointed the shotgun at the wispy, older man, the book-keeper.

'You step up to the counter.'

Jasper finished with the window-blind, turned on the balls of his feet, crossed to the counter, vaulted across it gun in hand, fished forth a flour sack and shoved it at the old man with a command. 'Fill it. Empty out all them drawers along here. You miss a dollar, mister, and I'll kill you.'

Jasper did not wait to supervise, he headed towards the rear of the room, reached the door back there and unbolted it, left it hanging ajar, and cast one peek outward. Abel was idling out there in the sunshine, his back to the building, looking up and down the empty alleyway. Jasper turned back.

Roy Eastman sauntered to the counter where the aged bookkeeper, with beads of transparent sweat on his forehead, worked with clumsy fingers, leaned the shotgun there pointing directly at Charles Monmouth's stomach, both dogs hauled all the way back, one thick finger curled around the foremost trigger. A good scattergun-man could detonate both barrels of his weapon by tugging off the foremost trigger then, as the recoil jammed the weapon backward, allowing the same finger to slide back and tug the second trigger. The noise was deafening, but more significant, two full-bore barrels fired like that from a sawed-off shotgun, scattered pellets in a wide pattern that could completely dismember anyone in front of the gun.

'I'd like to make a withdrawal,' he said quietly, looking directly at Monmouth. 'Open the safe.'

Monmouth nodded. 'I got to turn around, Mr Johnson.'

Eastman nodded. 'Then turn around, Mr Monmouth.' He did not take his eyes off the three men by the safe as he said, 'Jasper; the gun . . .'

There was always at least one sixgun inside a bank safe. There was not always someone courageous — or rash — enough to reach for it, though. Jasper stepped to one side, not in Eastman's way but able to see into the safe over Monmouth's shoulder.

There was not a sound throughout the building as Charles Monmouth worked the combination-lock. Outside, someone called a greeting to someone else out there, from the centre of the roadway, and booted feet scuffing across the plankwalk made a dull-sounding echo as Monmouth swung the big door back with an effort. Jasper rammed his cocked Colt into Monmouth's side.

'Get out of the way,' he ordered, and Monmouth stepped sideways.

Jasper saw the gun, reached for it, shoved it into his waistband, then holstered his own weapon as he brought forth another small flour sack and went to work systematically cleaning out the safe. He touched only money. There was a drawer of jewellery and several string-tied bundles of bonds, he no more than glanced at either one.

The old man had gone down the counter behind each wicket and had his flour sack stuffed with currency. As he looked up, shaking, Eastman gestured, and held out one hand. The bookkeeper walked up and passed over the sack. Eastman pointed the shotgun at him. 'Over there with the others.'

As the old man crossed the room Eastman stepped to the little swinging gate, passed inside and leaned, shotgun in one hand, flour-sack full of money in the other hand. He and Charles Monmouth looked steadily at one another. Monmouth was white to the hairline. The kind of loss his bank was going to suffer this day, would force the doors closed. His troubles were only just beginning; bank managers had been lynched for allowing something like this to happen. Those that managed to leave a town where their bank had been cleaned out, rarely ever got another job in any bank, anywhere.

Monmouth was not armed, but he had a Colt in his desk-drawer. He was about thirty feet from the desk, and even if he'd been able to reach the weapon, he knew absolutely that he would be no match for the bearded man in the duster, who handled that heavy scattergun gun-handed.

Jasper pulled open little drawers, sifted through the contents with his left hand seeking additional money, then finally stepped back leaving the safe gutted and in total disarray. He knotted the top of his flour sack, shoved it inside his shirt, pulled the pistol from his waistband, cocked it and stepped across in front of the three witnesses. None of them moved so much as a finger.

The entire robbery had not taken ten minutes, but out front someone knocked on the door as though the robbery had taken longer. This was one of those risks that had to be taken. As a rule, *something* happened. Seldom was it any more critical than this, but nevertheless it happened. You couldn't upset established routines without some kind of precedent interrupting, even though for the most part it was no more important than an impatient depositor out front wanting to enter.

Eastman shoved his flour sack inside his shirt, also, then he gestured with the scattergun. 'Mr Monmouth, walk to your desk.' The moment Monmouth turned, Jasper's gun swung in a short, chopping arc.

Monmouth's body fell sideways, striking the high table of the bookkeeper.

Eastman swung the scattergun to Billings. 'You next,' he said. Billings hung slack for a moment, until Jasper reached and gave him a shove, then chopped him down too. He did that three times. The last man to fall was the aged bookkeeper. He closed his eyes tightly and at the very last second, flinched. The gunbarrel struck down alongside his head tearing his ear half off, but at that the old man was fortunate. He bled like a stuck hog but his brittle old skull which might have burst under Jasper's gunbarrel, remained intact as he fell.

Jasper flung the gun down and stepped to the rear doorway. Whoever that was out front was banging on the door now with his fist, impatient still, but also angry now.

Eastman was the last one through the rear door. He turned, glanced around, then jumped through and ran for his horse. Abel was waiting, holding the animal. Jasper was already astraddle leather whirling his animal. The moment Eastman was in the saddle, Abel vaulted upon his mount and called to Jasper as he led the way through the alley to a vacant lot where people had been flinging refuse for a long while. Abel picked his way through until they were upon a paralleling residential roadway, then he turned a little until he reached a less hazardous vacant site, and hooked his animal with both spurs.

They left Sioux Falls riding fast, which perhaps was not necessary, and in fact might have attracted attention, but experience had taught them that riding slowly out of a town, while it aroused no one, sacrificed time, which was the only thing more valuable after robbing a town, than losing one of the flour sacks.

The sun was slightly off-centre overhead, the land lay open and sparkling-clear on all sides of them, but miles deep, in the direction of those badlands, there was a distance-haze. They rode directly towards it without even looking back until they were miles away and slackened pace a little, in order to save their horses, which were the only other assurance they had; distance and reliable mounts were what they had to rely on from this point onward. There would be pursuit, of course, and they could be tracked, but if they had enough open country and mounts which were as good or better than anything their pursuers had, they would make it. They knew tricks for eluding pursuit, but unless their animals were in top shape, when the chase settled down to a steady, grim race, all the tricks in the world would not save them. Men who had been cleaned out of all their savings did not give up nor forget.

Six miles out, with the badlands clearly in sight ahead, Eastman slowed to a walk, fished out his flour sack and peered into it. Abel said, 'What's it look like, Roy?'

Jasper answered when Eastman did not. 'That damned safe was full of money. I wish to gawd we'd dared haul along . . . Roy, there was three rows of gold pouches in there.'

Eastman looped his reins, ignored the other two and thumbed back his hat, then began pulling out greenbacks and counting them with an expression of total concentration. When he was finished he looked up with a detached smile. 'Four thousand dollars, by gawd. Give me your bag, Jasper.' He handed over his counted money as Jasper obeyed, then he untied the knot and began pulling out that money as well.

The greenbacks from Jasper's sack were in larger denominations. Evidently Charles Monmouth did not like having the large notes at the tellers' wickets. Eastman chuckled mid-way through his counting, this time, and when he finished he lit a cigar and beamed on his partners.

'By gawd we done it this time,' he announced.

Abel's excitement was obvious. 'How much, then, damn it all?'

'Eight thousand in Jasper's sack.'

They looked at one another. Twelve thousand dollars! The world was full of men who worked all their grubbing damned lousy lives and never made that much, and there were even *more* men in the world who had never in their lives *seen* that much money.

'Split,' said Abel, and Eastman counted it out from both sacks, made three divisions and passed it out. Then, folding the two flour sacks, he handed them back to Jasper, twisted in the saddle to look back, saw nothing as far back as it was possible for him to see in the direction of Sioux Falls, and settled forward still wearing that easy, dispassionate smile, as he smoked his cigar and rode straight up in the saddle.

Abel's excitement was leashed for as long as it took him to recount his share of the money. Afterwards he reared back and let go with a whoop, then he too looked back. There was nothing back there, no sign of horsemen, not even any dust. 'This time,' he said, 'I'm goin' all the way back to my hometown. Chriz' a'mighty, a man could fairly well kill himself pleasuring with this kind of money.'

'Yeah,' retorted Jasper dryly, 'and he could *get* himself killed too, spending it wild and making folks suspicious. A robbery like we just done will be in every newspaper from here to there, and back again. There'll be lawmen comin' to life in every damned city and village. They'll offer rewards too. Abel, you better not go home, you'd do better to go somewhere else, maybe down to Messico for a few months.'

Jasper knew his man; Abel had been born reckless. He'd no more be able to restrain himself with that much money in his pockets, than he'd be able to fly.

Roy Eastman rode along hardly listening. *This* time he'd made it; this time he'd got enough in one robbery to do almost anything he wanted to do. He had always believed that, someday, somewhere, he'd get more money from a bank than he could stuff in all his pockets at the same time.

Chapter Ten

THE LONG RIDE BEGINS

What the sod-buster, Joshua Barnard, had said about the badlands was correct, up to a point, but evidently, if Barnard had ever visited that country at all, he had not explored it very extensively; it was even better for the purpose of outlaws in flight than Barnard had implied, or than Roy Eastman had suspected.

There was precious little livestock feed for the first three or four miles. The land was rocky, arid, split and cracked, and where the rock ledges protruded like old bones, the land looked shattered and up-ended. No wonder the cattlemen did not turn animals in there; even if there had been a little feed, it still would have been one hell of a place to try and round up animals.

Eastman canted slightly towards the north, riding at a steady walk as he did this. There were some genuine mountains off in that direction. If he could lose the pursuit in the rocky badlands, and reach those greener distant mountains, he could put Dakota

Territory behind him.

They always had a few flat tins of food along, and as a rule water was no problem in the northwest, at least it was no problem until late autumn when waterholes dried up. This was late spring, or early summer, whichever way folks cared to view it.

They found better feed for the animals after they had begun angling northward, and while they were still in the badlands. It was this windfall which convinced Eastman that Joshua Barnard hadn't really done much exploring over in the badlands.

They found the best feed in a low place, a sort of circular, sunken big depression which was the only such area in all the badlands. Whatever had punched that big depression in the ground had also ruptured a watervein a few feet below ground level; there was a little clear-water pond to one side of this fifty-acre circular hole.

This is where they finally dismounted, off-saddled, carefully washed their horses' backs, made certain the animals got over where the graze was best, then they went to taste the water. It was cold and sweet. As Eastman arose, his dirty old linen duster dragging in some mud, and wiped his bearded mouth as he turned to look back in the direction they had come, he said,

'There's a herd of awful mad folks back there in Sioux Falls by now, gents.'

Jasper shed his hat and shirt, sluiced off in the cold water, and smiled when the other two men stood staring; that water was like ice. In fact, when they hunkered to enjoy their meagre meal, Jasper's mood was better than usual.

Four thousand dollars in a man's pockets made a lot of difference, in the dourest of men.

They had no map. They never used maps, they used sight, and directional orientation, which was built-in to each one of them, and a rather general, sound knowledge of how land lay and how it changed. You didn't need a map to lose yourself in the wilds, all you needed was the wilds, and some idea of where the boundaries were.

Montana was northward, Wyoming was southward, Idaho and Oregon were in another direction, and easterly, beyond the cow country of Nebraska, lay the States. Otherwise, despite the railroads and the telegraph wires which had both pushed as far as Dakota Territory in some places, there was still all the empty land a trio of outlaws would need to hide in, for as long as they chose to remain in hiding.

Eastman left his partners napping in the

benign warmth of the depression and sauntered back a mile to a slight, stony outcrop-
ping, where he sat down with the old duster
sagging all around him, and shaded his eyes
to establish a long vigil. He was fairly certain
the pursuit would be unable to locate shod-
horse signs once the Eastman gang had
gotten into the rocky country. At least, if
they happened to have a bloodhound along
or maybe an Indian tracker, and actually *did*
find the trail and keep to it, they would have
to progress very slowly through the
rockfields, and when daylight failed they
would have to either dry-camp where they
were and await dawn, or turn back, and
either way the Eastman gang would be
moving through the night, widening the distance.

He was satisfied, not just with the success
of the robbery, which had gone off perfectly.
Even those three damned women who had
been in there when he'd unlimbered the
scattergun, had frozen in place against the
front wall and had not seemed even to
breathe. Otherwise, no one had been shot,
the money had been more than any of them
had dared hope, and their escape had gone
off very well too. They had the best horses.
They had all the land they would ever need
to manoeuvre in, and they had such a head-

start that try as he might, right at this moment, he could not, even yet, detect movement back in the direction of Sioux Falls. There was a thin spindrift of dust northward, up above Sioux Falls in the direction of the stageroad. It could be a posse riding in the wrong direction, but more probably it was a band of rangeriders from some outlying cow-outfit boiling into town after having heard of the robbery. Or, of course, it could simply be a stage running southward on a routine schedule.

He lit another cigar, sat up there on the warm rock making a steady, long study of the countryside, and turned just once to look off in the direction of the depression. He could see their horses browsing, but he could not see down where the men were sleeping, at all.

He felt perfectly relaxed and at ease. In all his years beyond the law, he had only had everything work out exactly as he wanted it to, perhaps six or eight times, and of all those times he had never raided a bank of more than five or six thousand dollars, which, when it was split three ways, was better pay than a man could make cowboying or homesteading, but it still lacked a lot of being enough to allow a man to really feel independent. *Now,* he felt independent.

He never planned ahead. He had stopped doing that when he finally had to stand in the middle of his Idaho claim and look around at everything he had had such great hopes and plans for, knowing that he was irredeemably defeated. There *was* no future. There would have been if his wife had remained; a man by himself naturally let down, but a man with responsibility never let down; he'd keep plodding and straining like a blind mule, until they patted him in the face with a shovel. A man with a family had a *reason* — had a reason even to do pointless, useless things, just as long as he kept trying. A man by himself . . .

'Hey; you daydreaming?'

It was Abel, with a cigarette dangling from his loose mouth. He was hatless, his shirt was unbuttoned at the top to disclose golden-pale hair on his powerful chest, loose-moving and serene in the face. He paused, standing erect looking outward.

'See anything?' he asked.

Eastman removed the cigar to reply. 'No. Some dust miles off northwestward, but it's gone now. Maybe was some riders, or a stage, or someone driving cattle, anyway, it was in the wrong direction and a hell of a distance off.'

Abel squatted down, hooked long arms

over his elbows and smoked for a while, squinting out over the badlands. He wagged his head gently. 'Old Janicek is going to have his best laugh in years, tonight. He hated 'em all, in Sioux Falls.'

Eastman was not interested in old Janicek, nor in old Barnard, nor in anyone else, right at this moment, unless they appeared on horseback with a gun, from the direction of the town. He moved slightly to find a better sitting spot; the kind of grey, smooth rock that made up this worthless badlands country was as unyielding as flint.

'We'll make a big sashay,' he told Abel. 'Up into the mountains northward, then bear around easterly for a while, maybe fifteen or twenty miles, then cut around southward. From that point on, Abel, I reckon we'll split up.'

The younger man sat and thought about this for a while before saying, 'I got to thinking, back there when I come awake, Roy; it went off so good this time our luck's got to be runnin' strong.' He turned his head. 'There's a town called Fargo down-country a-ways, and according to the bohunk I stayed with, they got not one bank down there, they got two of them.' Abel studied the older man's calm, dark profile for a moment, but you could never read the face of a man with a full beard, so in the end he gave up trying and said, 'Like I just told you, with our luck running so good, and all, Roy . . .'

Eastman smoked complacently watching the sun drop lower and change from orange to pale red. When daylight failed, the last immediate danger would fail along with it. Right now, their best friend would be night-fall. He sighed, removed the stogie and said, 'Your pockets can't hold no more money, Abel. Besides, we kicked the hornet's nest back there. You ride into any damned town for the next couple of weeks, being a stranger and all, let alone being *three* strangers whose descriptions right down to their damned horses will be in everyone's mind, and even if you was as innocent as the driven snow, I wouldn't give a plugged cent for your chances.' He put a steady, sceptical gaze upon the younger man. 'Abel; once we split off you do what you want to do.' What Eastman was thinking was that once they split off, he would never see Abel again. Sure as night followed day Abel was going to do something reckless or thoughtless or rash, and get himself killed. Not that Eastman gave a damn. He was about half of a mind never to allow Abel to ride with him again, anyway.

Nothing more was said. After a while they drifted back and found Jasper working over his saddle, bareheaded and fresh-shaved even though the only water to wash or shave with was in that ice-water pool across the hollow. He glanced up, then jutted his jaw Indian-fashion to a little ring of stones with a small fire burning in the middle of it. There was a little dented pan on the stones with the wonderful aroma of boiling coffee arising from it.

Eastman liked that. As he walked over and knelt down, the old linen coat dragging in the dirt, he could not avoid making a thoughtful comparison between them. The 'breed was a better man to ride with than Abel ever would be.

They had their coffee, one cup each because the pan was too small for more than that, then they brought in the horses just ahead of full dusk, saddled up, struck camp, rode up out of their depression and paused upon the northward rim to look back one more time.

'Dust,' said Jasper, spitting the word out.

He was correct. There was a fair-sized cloud of it, too, coming due east towards the farthest boundary of the badlands from the direction of Sioux Falls.

Abel made a dry comment. ' 'Bout time

them slow bastards got off their butts.'

Eastman had one comment to make. He sat and studied the dust, then lifted his rein-hand to move off. 'They won't even find the camp until tomorrow,' he said, and settled his old hat more comfortably on the back of his head as he faced forward scanning the country into which they would now ride.

Dusk closed down, bringing all the distance in closer. An hour after they left the depression it was no longer possible to see as far off as that posse's dust had been. They could see a mile or two ahead, but that eventually got whittled down until their visibility was no more than a few hundred yards.

But the country did not really break up for a number of miles yet. It was uneven, up-ended, ragged and crumbly right up until their horses' shoes stopped grating over rock and began sinking an inch or two into the soft, warm soil of the far foothills. By the time this happened they were many miles northeastward of their camp. By then, too, full night was down over the entire Territory. Eastman rode slouched and easy. The younger men on both sides of him were just as relaxed. Several times Abel offered to start a conversation but he did not get much response so, after a while, even Abel rode in silence.

They smelled the forest before they were close enough to make out the dark bulk of it. Up here, Eastman remarked, they would leave tracks a child could follow. The answer to this situation was movement. As long as possemen had to keep going, had to keep riding on someone's back-trail, they were not going to come up with the men making the trail. Where outlaws got into trouble — often *fatal* trouble — was when they thought they had put so many miles between themselves and the pursuit, that, tracks or no tracks, they could haul off and lie down for a night's sleep. Eastman knew better.

He kept pressing along eastward at the base of the high mountains. He could have meandered up through the trees and made it harder for the pursuit to pick up his sign, but riding in an unfamiliar forest at night-time slowed men too much.

There was a moon, but it couldn't penetrate that miles-deep stand of enormous pine and fir trees, though it helped them make their way as long as they remained just southward, out upon the more open country of the rolling foothills.

The horses were equal to all this. They had done it a number of times before, and between times they had rested amply. Most important of all, they were young and strong and sound as new money, the only kind of horses men rode who made a profession of out-riding other men.

It turned cold, eventually, which was how they all knew it was late, perhaps midnight or later. Eastman did not allow a stop except once, when they came to a creek, and watered the horses.

Jasper rode stoically, grey eyes turned black beneath the bent brim of his hat, sturdy body absorbing every slight jolt of the horse under him. Abel rode loose too, but Abel looked out and around from time to time as though in search of a good place to make camp. He did not mention halting, though. Like Jasper, he had been riding with Roy Eastman long enough to know that when it was safe for them to halt, Eastman would let them know.

Eastman was an enigma to Abel. More so to Abel, in fact, than he was to Jasper, although the 'breed did not really understand Eastman either. The difference was that the 'breed did not try very hard to understand Roy Eastman; in his own way, Jasper was just as detached, as inward, as Roy Eastman was, but it had not happened the same way for either of them. Jasper's fatalism was something inherent, Eastman's fatalism was somehow tied up with a complete refusal to think about the day after tomorrow. He would just keep riding until, one day, he would no longer be able to keep riding.

Chapter Eleven

A LONG RIDE

It was four in the morning, cold and paling, out along the farthest curve of the earth, when Eastman hauled up in a grassy place with the forest no more than arm's reach on their left, dismounted stiffly and wordlessly hobbled his horse before off-saddling.

Afterwards they built a little fire and hunkered close to it with saddleblankets round their shoulders. Men with a little grease under their hides could stand cold a lot better than men who had none. Also, if they'd had food in their bellies, which could have fuelled their inner heat-generating capabilities, the cold wouldn't have bothered them so much. In any case, they were all shivering by the time Eastman decided it was safe to halt for a while and make a fire.

It took almost a full hour for the bone-deep chill to depart, making way for a wonderfully pleasant sense of warm well-being. Jasper eventually went in search of water to make coffee with, and was fortunate enough to find some. Then they sat a little less stiffly, basking in the heat and savouring the aroma of the heating coffee.

Abel rolled a cigarette, Eastman lit a stogie, and Jasper sat poking small twigs into the fire to keep heat coming back to him.

Eastman was studying his partners when he said, 'You got to do *something* to earn it, even when you steal it.'

Jasper raised grey eyes and Eastman grinned at him. 'This ain't a hardship,' said Jasper. 'Chriz; I was raised believing things like this was the *good* times.'

When the coffee was ready they drank it, and that helped too. It was a good thing they managed to get warm, because, as the new day dawned, the cold became much more intense, as it always did, summer or winter, just before sun-up. They would have felt it more this morning.

They kept their fire going, even increased the size of it once the sky paled out, because, aside from their knowledge that the posse was back down-country too far to see flames, with the advent of early morning the flames would lose their brilliance. In daylight, men never saw a fire, they saw its *smoke*. It was the wrong time of the day for that, too. Pre-dawn was the *colour* of smoke.

Eastman, lolling back, pleasantly warm and relaxed, said, 'Sure could enjoy a breakfast steak about now, with a bowl of hash-browned spuds on the side, a big piece of apple or berry pie.'

Jasper laughed when Abel groaned and rolled up his eyes. Then Abel also laughed. 'Why not make it a Thanksgivin' turkey with all the fixings? Roy, as long as you ain't going to get no wish anyway, why not wish for the best?'

Eastman's rare jocular mood continued. 'All right, I'll wish for a turkey with stuffin', and pumpkin pie, and buttermilk, squash, and fresh-baked bread . . .' He looked at the younger men. 'What am I forgettin'?'

'Coffee,' said Abel, and Jasper simply shrugged and poked more twigs into the fire, then looked out where their horses were, with a soft-sad expression across his face.

'Coffee,' conceded Eastman, savouring his stogie between comments. 'By gawd we'll all have it like that *this* year. If we don't it'll be our own damned fault.'

Abel pitched his cigarette butt into their fire. 'You know what they're goin' to do to us if they catch us?' he asked, changing everyone's mood with his question. 'They're going to —'

'First,' spoke up Eastman, curtly, 'they got to catch us.' He flicked ash before continuing. 'We'll keep together until tomorrow morning. By then I figure we'd ought to be fifty more miles northeastward. By then we can safely split up.' He smiled. 'What does a posse do when it runs across three *separate* sets of tracks, where it's been followin' one set? And that's providin' those townsmen aren't all rubbed raw from all this unaccustomed riding. I never yet seen a town posse that was worth a good gawddamn.'

Abel yawned, then nodded in agreement with some part of Eastman's statement; for all the others knew, he agreed with all of it despite that earlier moment of gloom, or whatever had inspired him to change the subject when they'd been joking about the meals they would like.

Jasper had been sitting quietly tending the fire, listening, and keeping his own counsel. Now, as he shoved in a branch, he said, 'We meet next summer down in Denver again?'

Eastman was looking at Abel when Jasper spoke. He was annoyed, not by the question, but by the *timing* of the question. He had just about made up his mind that even if Abel managed not to get caught or killed between now and next summer, he did not

121

want Abel riding with him again. He could find another man; there were always plenty of *those* around. He finished the stogie and dropped it into the fire, then straightened up where he'd been lolling and gazed for a moment into the flames before answering. Abel was waiting, as was Jasper, so he said, 'Yeah, I reckon,' then he removed the saddleblanket from his shoulders and prepared to arise. The new-day light was bright enough now so that visibility was much improved. He did not want either of them to pursue this topic, so he got stiffly to his feet and stretched, then looked out where the horses were still cropping grass, and said, 'Might as well dust it.'

An idea had come to him as he'd sat there looking into the fire. He would go back up to Kalispell in the early spring and meet Jasper before Jasper saddled up for the long ride down to Denver. *Then,* he would explain about Abel, and they would not go to Denver, but would head out in a different direction, and somewhere along the trail they'd pick up the third man they'd need. Abel could sit the summer out in Denver, if he chose, or he could take a riding job, or, for all Eastman cared, he could try to recruit a gang of his own and go raiding.

They saddled up, mounted, and left the

comfortable little warm place with all its tranquillity, heading up closer to the edge of the forest this time; men riding across an empty land were easily spotted — unless their moving was masked by an uneven, busy background.

The cold lingered, but when the sun finally arose, the outlying, flat country warmed up. This helped a little although forested highlands did not really turn warm until along towards mid-day. Any place where the sun could not burn through, remained chilly even in summertime.

By mid-day when they watered the horses at a creek, hunger was beginning to be more than something to joke about. Coffee was fine, but after their meagre supply of tinned food was exhausted, even coffee was a poor substitute for something solid.

Rawhide-tough men could go a surprisingly long time between meals, though. No one mentioned food until, with the sun almost directly above them, Eastman saw a small stone dam across a little brawling watercourse, and stopped to sit his saddle looking at the stones. No beaver had made that. In fact, no four-legged animal of any kind, had made it. He looked left and right, saw the trail he sought, and wordlessly turned his horse up it.

They emerged into a small clearing, man-made, where a trapper-cabin, a sort of three-sided lean-to affair, had been erected of notched logs. Whoever the pelt-hunter was, he only intended to use his lean-to after the worst of winter was past, otherwise he'd have closed in the front, made a fire-ring inside, and he would also have chinked between the logs.

Nevertheless, they scouted the surrounding area for fresh signs, then came together again out front of the cabin and dismounted. The trapper hadn't been around for months, evidently.

Eastman said, 'Look up the trees for his cache.'

They scattered out on foot. Jasper found it and sang out. The trapper had pulled two saplings close, had roped them into place, had made a platform up there, and the bundle was lashed up there covered with a rotting old dirty piece of waxed tarpaulin.

They got the cache down, opened it, and found exactly what they needed. In fact, when Abel opened a tin which turned out to hold peaches, it developed that they had found something much more, and much better, than they expected, or needed.

Everyone's mood improved as they gorged themselves. Abel said, 'The Lord takes care of his own,' and laughed. 'When the trapper comes back next year he's going to be mad as a hornet.'

Jasper agreed, and added a little more. 'Mad's only part of it. He'll know damned well didn't no bear get his cache.'

After they were full as ticks, they divided the remaining tins and stowed them in their saddlebags. They now had more than enough food to last them until each one of them got down to civilization again.

If they hadn't found that cache they wouldn't have starved. Three armed men who had matured on the frontier would not starve as long as they were in a country that had a dozen varieties of game in it. But this way, as Eastman observed, they did not have to fire a shot — and risk having the report heard miles off by someone who might be curious enough to try and find the shooter.

Afterwards, they lay back in the grass like torpid snakes, sopping up sunlight-warmth while their animals grazed off the little clearing, which, at its best, could only produce enough feed for one animal for about two or three days. Three animals ate the grass down in a matter of hours.

They slept hard until near mid-afternoon when a flight of camp-robbers coming in to roost in some nearby trees saw them and set up such a scolding Eastman was awakened with a pounding heart; bluejays only made a lot of noise when intruders were near. For a moment he did not realize *they* were the intruders; that there was no one else around.

He roused Abel and Jasper. They went sluggishly to saddle up and ride on. The warmth stayed with them, this time, even though they rode into the forest, but as soon as sundown approached, the warmth would depart again.

They did not talk much now; they were well fed, warmed up, and the only thing remaining for them to do was the same thing they had been doing for twenty-four hours now — ride. That was their second nature; it did not inspire conversation. In vast country a horse was simply an extension of a man's shorter, and fewer, legs. When the horses under them were willing and able, and when the men had already exhausted all the practical talk, unless they turned frivolous there was really little to be said. Excepting Abel, none of them were frivolous, except very rarely, and even Abel's ebullient spirit was not that way this afternoon.

They did not go very far northward into the trees. All they required of the forest was that it provide them with protective screening, which it did just as well at the lower elevations as it could have done up higher, and if they had climbed higher it would have taxed the horses.

Eastman had been at this sort of thing too many years not to realize that his horse was all that stood between him and disaster, once the manhunt for him was on. He kept to the lower slope, passing in and out of the trees, perfectly calm and relaxed, perfectly confident. As he said, the more they rode, the farther they went, the longer they kept at it, tiresome as all this might be, the less their chances of being overhauled.

They had not seen dust from that Sioux Falls' posse at all, since the afternoon before. It was possible the posse was still doggedly back there, in the trees, too, where it would make no dust either, but Eastman did not consider that a very strong possibility. He considered being overhauled by a band of store-clerks, town blacksmiths and the like, even less of a possibility.

When they came to a more open part of the mountains, still bearing eastward, and Jasper detected a stageroad far ahead, which indicated there had to be a settlement of some sort down there, Roy Eastman was even tempted to go seek the town and buy a decent hot meal and maybe a bottle. But he did not mention this; if he had, Abel would have come to life, and afterwards Abel would have harped upon it for hours as they continued riding in the direction of the stageroad.

Jasper saw several riders on the lower plain and pointed them out. They appeared to be rangeriders, perhaps looking for strayed horses or cattle. They were loping slowly in the direction of the stageroad, which roughly paralleled the course of the Eastman gang.

Abel said, 'We're gettin' into new country, Roy. Good thing they got no telegraphs up here.' He stood in the stirrups, one hand on the cantle, looking back. Eastman smiled.

'If you're looking for that Sioux Falls' posse, Abel, you'll be lookin' for a long time. Even if they can read our signs, they'll be miles back. You can't ride fast in a forest, especially when the tracks aren't worth a damn that you're following.'

Chapter Twelve

A DAWNING SUSPICION

If they had been farther back closer to the Sioux Falls cow-country, Roy would have avoided all that open, grassy country where the forest thinned out east of the stageroad, but he was confident, and he was becoming more confident with each passing hour.

But he baulked at the idea of going down the road, when they were almost up to it, in search of a town. Abel mentioned doing this and Jasper looked wryly at him; Jasper knew exactly what Eastman would say.

'You do what you want after we split up tomorrow morning, Abel, but until then we'll ride *my* way, and we don't go town-hunting.'

Abel persisted, exactly as Eastman had thought he might. 'For Chriz' sake, Roy, we got to be at least sixty, maybe eighty miles northeast of Sioux Falls. We don't have to do more'n maybe belly up to a bar for a few rounds, then hike on out again.'

If Abel had used almost any example but that one. Eastman looked at him, and even

Jasper put a grey-eyed, stony stare his way. Abel recognized his error and swore, not at the others, at himself, and that ended his argument about riding down the stageroad until they came to the edge of it, and halted to look up and around, then he leaned on the saddlehorn peering southward, out where the town would be, if there was one, and made a deliberate, loud groan, which Eastman ignored as he inched his horse the last hundred feet and slid it with stiff forelegs down the crumbly bank to the hard-packed gritty roadway.

North of them there were several horsemen up the slope. It looked like that same band they had seen earlier, and had thought might be cowboys out stray-hunting. Evidently those men were travellers. Eastman shrugged that off and looked elsewhere.

Northward, and perhaps three miles on eastward, but farther up along a low spine-top where a few wind-twisted trees stood, there was a thin-standing spiral of dark smoke. Jasper tipped back his hat as he studied this phenomenon. 'If I didn't know better,' he said, 'I'd guess it was In'ians smoking meat up there.'

Eastman nodded. 'Yeah. If you didn't know better. Be a damned dumb In'ian who'd build a meat-drying fire plumb a-top a ridge like that, for everyone to see. Anyway, from what I've heard, there aren't too many In'ians still in Dakota Territory, and them as stayed, wear pants and ride saddles, and either punch cows or hang out in the saloons — where it's allowed.'

Jasper continued to study the smoke, but when Roy continued on across the road, Jasper shrugged and joined his partners.

They had now crossed an immense uninhabited terrain, and as Abel had said, they were in a different place. Normally, that would have meant something, but not now; not to men who had stolen all the savings a lot of other men had sweated and strained and gone-without to accumulate, over a lot of years. This was something that rode right along with them as though there had been a fourth horseman in the party.

The fresh country seemed more like the Sioux Falls area than anything else they'd traversed, or would traverse, because it had cattle in it, and a town somewhere southward out of sight, and rangeriders, and even a north-to-south stageroad.

Eastman could *feel* the nearness of people without actually seeing any more of them than those riders who had gone up the roadway towards the top-out which lay sharp against the pale, flawless blue sky.

He didn't worry, because now, finally, their hard-riding would be a great advantage. No one could have preceded them, and even the pursuit, if it was still back there, couldn't reach this new country until perhaps tonight, and by then the darkness would be their ally again. And in the morning, if folks were looking for three riders, they wouldn't see but one horseman passing through. They would split up come firstlight, tomorrow.

The mountains were not as wooded, over in this territory, nor were they as steep nor bulky. They seemed to curve back around as though some ancient sea had washed hard against them in an eddying way, worrying away thousands of tons of earth, and leaving this cupped-shaped, low-ridged, shallow-bulked residue behind, as the ancient sea had receded.

They had to cross open country as they clung to the south slope. There were no thick stands of timber even back up near the top-out, and there were little bands of far cattle up in here. Every now and then they started up a bunch, which fled, tails high, at sight of horsemen. It hadn't been too long ago that these cattle had been at a marking-ground, and they remembered, especially the younger steer calves — who had been bulls the last time they had seen mounted men; they fled the fastest and farthest, not able to understand in their dumb-brute minds, that a man couldn't do *that* to them but once.

Eastman sniffed smoke and paused to look around. Jasper pointed. 'Them fellers up yonder on the rim,' he said, still puzzled by why anyone would be smoking meat — if they were Indians up there — or doing anything else with fire a-top a bony low ridge, this time of day. Jasper dropped his arm and sat squinting in the direction of the smoke. 'It's no lightning-strike,' he opined, more to himself, in his bafflement, than to his companions, 'and it sure as hell ain't In'ians. And no one'd have a branding fire a-top a damned mountain. What are they *doing* up there?'

Roy looked, then reined out again, eastward. 'It don't concern us,' he said, his dark gaze fixed on around the concave mountainside towards the place, miles distant, where the mountain became a mountain again, forested and dark, and bulking-vast.

'We'll find a campsite yonder,' he told his companions. 'It'll be safe to make a decent fire tonight.' He looked around and gave that detached smile of his. 'Tonight, we'll eat tinned peaches from the cache, and get a good night's rest, then, come morning, we'll split off.'

Roy hadn't been really worried since they'd first fled from Sioux Falls. The fact that the pursuit hadn't even got astride for hours after the robbery, had diminished his worry until, by last night around their little coffee-fire, he hadn't even felt hunted, which was something he usually felt even when he thought he was probably safe. Now, with another night and a lot more miles behind him, he scarcely more than glanced up now and then, where that spin-drift of dark smoke was rising. It *was* an un-likely place for a branding-fire, or even for a camp — a-top a wind-swept rim — but whatever they were doing up there couldn't possibly have any bearing on the Eastman gang.

They were at the deepest inward-curve of their concave mountainside when Abel raised in the saddle, twisting to look back-wards, and let go with a harsh curse. He did not straighten forward, either, he continued to look back as he said, 'Who in hell's behind us?'

Roy stopped and looked. So did Jasper. There were several riders back there, some of them higher along the concave slope, several lower down, and all of them riding in the same direction as the Eastman gang. But riding slowly, loosely, as though they might be scouting the underbrush and sparse trees, and little swales, for lost cattle, which they could have been doing, except that to three outlaws on the run, there was an unmistakable chill in that sight. That happened to also be the way manhunting possemen rode.

'Cowboys,' said Roy Eastman, making it sound very matter-of-fact. 'We seen cattle up in here. That's what they're lookin' for.'

Abel sat forward with a fervent: 'I sure *hope* that's what they're lookin' for,' and joined the other two as they continued on their eastward way.

Jasper rolled a cigarette, lit it, broke the sulphur-stick and flung it down, raked the countryside with a grey stare, and ended up watching that ropey spiral of smoke up yonder. Meanwhile, they crossed a shale-rock opening among the trees where only some kind of thorny underbrush grew, and passed back into stirrup-high grass again, before Jasper suddenly grunted and hauled back on his reins, staring up the mountain towards the ridge.

'Gawddammit,' he exclaimed, and spat out his cigarette. 'They're *signalling*, Roy!'

Eastman and Abel also halted. Roy frowned. 'What are you talking about?'

Jasper raised a thick arm, rigidly pointing. 'Damn it, use your eyes and look up there. Those fellers are using their smoke to make some kind of signals. Watch, now. You see that puff of smoke? There; now there ain't none. Watch; there, you see it; another puff.' Jasper lowered his arm and gripped the saddlehorn. 'They're signalling from up there — and what in hell would they be doing that *for?*'

Abel craned upwards, his face wreathed with an expression of incredulity. 'Not about *us,*' he muttered. 'Hell's bells, they couldn't know about us over here, not for another day anyway.'

Eastman watched the dark puffs, then twisted in the saddle and squinted backwards. Those horsemen were still coming, and now they seemed to be closing the distance a little. He tried to count them, but it was hard to do through trees and underbrush, and they were scattered out, some ahead, some farther back, but he made an estimate as he swung ahead in the saddle. 'Eight or ten of them back there. Come along.' Eastman urged his mount onward again, controlling an urge to use speed. If they made a dash for the distant forest, which was still miles distant, it would look suspicious; they had to keep walking their horses.

He echoed Abel. 'It's not us, Jasper. It *can't* be. Not until maybe tonight at the earliest.'

Jasper's practical mind refuted this. 'You want to stake your life on that?' he demanded, and looked back, too. 'Those fellers aren't hunting cattle, Roy. If that was it, they wouldn't still be shagging us. There's cattle all around through here. They don't turn off, they just keep coming.'

Eastman's temper flared. Jasper was going to panic them all, if he kept this up. 'Damn you,' he said savagely, 'let me do the worrying. I tell you they can't be after us. There's no way they could have got word over here without a telegraph. Not even if they sent out a rider, he couldn't have covered as much ground as we've covered.'

A half hour later the smoke died, up a-top the ridge, and that was reassuring, although those horsemen were still coming, still closing the gap a little at a time, but without really pushing their horses. Evidently they, too, wanted it to appear they were just making a casual ride.

Eastman concentrated on the yonder mountains, which were a continuation of the same slopes they had been riding since last night, but which were not like the half-barren concave slope they had been crossing now, for the past few hours. If they could reach those trees by sundown, even if that was a posse back there, somehow or other, they could lose it in the darkness, in the forest.

Eastman worried, for the first time, even though he kept telling himself this was impossible; there were no horses in Dakota Territory that were the equal to *their* horses, and there were damned few men in the Territory, either, who could keep to the trail as long as *they* had done.

Come morning, and damn them, whoever they were, they'd have a fresh mystery — three separate trails.

Abel sighed loudly. When Jasper and Roy turned, Abel did not even point, he simply jutted his jaw southward. There were four riders down there, on the flats, passing in and out among some little knobbly knolls, keeping abreast of the Eastman gang. Abel's attitude was, for him, very unusual. He did not swear nor get excited nor start talking fast. He seemed to have become suddenly fatalistic.

'Ten behind us,' said Jasper, 'and four below us, keepin' even, Roy. *That's* what them sons of bitches on the ridge were signalling about. Don't tell me *they're* lookin' for strays *too*. I'll be damned if I know how they done it, but Roy, they got us boxed in.'

Eastman yanked down the ragged brim of his old hat to shield his eyes, and studied the four distant horsemen. From time to time he saw them look up the slope. But that *still* did not have to mean anything.

For a damned fact, they had been riding into new cow-country all morning. That had been obvious from the moment they saw the stageroad.

But the fear Roy Eastman had only felt six or eight times in his life as an outlaw, came now to close like rawhide round his heart. If those *weren't* cowboys simply doing their normal day's work, then by gawd Jasper was right, they *were* boxed in — in *three* directions, but dead ahead where the forest loomed a couple of miles onward, the way was open. He had to fight down a powerful urge to sink in the hooks and bust out for the trees in a belly-down run.

Chapter Thirteen

THE LAST MILE

A frightened man isn't much different from a worried man. Roy kept watching the riders who were paralleling them down on the flat country, and the same eight or ten who were still shagging their back-trail, and although he *wanted* his best, or worst, to believe this was all pure coincidence, that he and his companions were too suspicious, too fearful and wary, the paralysing slow fear that built up in his mind worried him so much he could not, right then anyway, even make a good decision.

Fortunately, he did not have to make one; there was only one way he and his companions could ride — the same direction they were travelling in, eastward towards the distant forest. There was nothing else they could do, unless they turned and rode abruptly back to ask those eight or ten men what the hell they were doing, up here, and that didn't make much sense, because if it *was* a posse back there, they wouldn't need any more encouragement than that, to start shooting, and if it *wasn't* a posse, those riders were going to start wondering why three strangers were so agitated and warlike.

Abel lifted the tie-down off his sixgun. Jasper, from the corner of his eye, saw this movement, and stared at Abel. Eastman had not seen this, was not looking to his right or left but was trying to estimate how much more mountainside they had to ride before reaching the trees.

Jasper did the same; he also reached down to tug loose the tie-down.

Gradually, Roy's shock diminished. He *still* was not convinced, but nonetheless, he was a wanted man, a *very much* wanted man, in fact, and he thought like one, so, riding along in the delightful sunshine, dirty, dusty-bearded, his old linen duster more soiled than ever, he began piecing the thing together, and eventually, with only about a mile and a half left before he reached the protection of the forest, he twisted to look back up where that signal-fire had been. The skyline was clean and empty, up there; *that* was what he had wondered about. He knew, now, where ten or twelve or fourteen men were, behind them and down below, keeping them from being able to bust back or break off into the flat, lower country where they could make a race of it, but, *where were those men who had been on the rim?*

A hunted man thought like a man*hunter.* He had to, in order to survive. If *he* had been on that ridge, and had seen the retreat cut off behind the Eastman gang, had seen the southward escape also cut off, he would lead his crew in the only direction which still lay open to the outlaws, he would take them along his damned ridge to the yonder forest, then he would lead them down through it until he was dead-ahead of the oncoming outlaws. *Then,* by gawd, the Eastman gang would *really* be boxed in.

Jasper said something Roy did not catch, but he turned away. Jasper had seen a horseman lope westward from the broken foothills over at the base of the forested slopes, and join those four men down below. Roy said, 'Well, damn it all, that'll be a feller from whoever's up in front of us, maybe bringing word that they got into place throughout the yonder trees and are settin' in there cocked and primed.'

Abel lifted his rein-hand as though to stop his horse. 'In front, too?'

Roy shrugged, fished for his last stogie and looped his reins calmly, to light up. He did not take his dark eyes off Abel as he did this, and as he said, 'Them boys that was minding the fire a-top the ridge, Abel . . .

142

Where would you go, if you was them, and knew who we are?'

Abel did not answer. Instead, he said, 'How do we get clear, Roy?'

There was no way to get clear, not by *riding* anyway. Eastman worked the cigar to one corner of his beartrap mouth and spoke around it. 'Depends on them, Abel. I still ain't altogether convinced they're after us. I just can't figure how they could have done it faster than *we* done it.'

Jasper turned a bitter eye towards Eastman. 'That don't matter, Roy. They *done* it, *that* matters. So, what do we do?'

'We ride right along like we been doing, until we're almost to them trees up ahead, and if they don't hail us, then they aren't after us. If they *do* hail us,' Eastman turned his bearded face with the dark eyes bright but deadly calm in that detached manner, and smiled at Jasper. 'The first son of a bitch who sings out at me, is going to get a sound-shot right between his lousy eyes, then we got to run for it like the devil himself was behind us. Split up and don't slack off and don't look back. Ride like you never rode before in your life. It'll work, believe me. I've been in this position before and I'm still around. You got all kinds of help in them trees . . . The only trouble will come if our horses been too long on the trail. Otherwise, do exactly like I do.'

Eastman checked ash on his cigar and did not face his companions again as he plugged the stogie back into his bitter-curled mouth. There was no damned way under the sun to get clear by riding. The nearest he had come to telling them this was when he had commented on the condition of their animals.

They had favoured the horses, and they were fine, strong animals, but also, they had been riding them for more than twenty-four hours on nothing but an occasional gutful of washy grass. There was not a horse living who could run for his life for miles on end, after what their horses had been through, and win out. Especially not against other horses who had just drifted up out of some damned town or some ranch corral, fresh as a green gourd, and strong.

That left the outlaws' last resort. Not many men could stand up and face blazing guns, and even the ones who had that kind of courage, would not normally do it when they knew there was another way to overcome an enemy without the risk of taking a bullet in the brisket. Those men, whoever they were and wherever they had come from, knew as well as Roy Eastman also knew, that the Sioux Falls bank-robbers had been in the saddle upon the same animals more than twenty-four hours. They were stockmen; they knew all they had to know about horses under saddle in that condition. They would not have to shoot it out with the Eastman gang, and they also knew *that*.

They had the numbers, and for all Roy knew, there were more cowmen and townsmen converging, after that crew on the ridge finished signalling. All they had to do was ride the Eastman outlaws down, together or one at a time.

Roy had survived several miraculous escapes, including the one where he'd deliberately jumped a good horse off a high cliff. Maybe he was supposed to survive a few more, including this surround, and make another legendary escape. He was willing to strain every muscle and sinew in the effort — because he had to.

It was that fundamental. He had to. All three of them had to.

Jasper said, 'They're playing cat and mouse, damn 'em.'

Roy, watching the forest up ahead for movement, answered without looking around. 'Yeah, and the longer they play it the worse off they're going to be. They know about the Eastman gang. They're not in any hurry to come within bullet range.'

Jasper looked quickly over at Roy, his grey eyes shades darker than normal. 'That ain't it. They're just poking along, herding us like a band of sheep, until they get us right up where they want us. Then the battle will start.'

Abel suddenly said, 'Damnation, I had it all figured out what I was going to do with my four thousand dollars.' He, too, was peering intently ahead towards the forest. 'Roy; you figured I was going back home and cut a big fat hog in the butt, didn't you, drinkin' and dancin' and raising hell. I wasn't. I had in mind going to a place I know of down in west Texas and buying me a piece of land where I could be respectable, and maybe buy stolen Messican cattle and hold 'em on grass until they got greasy, then re-sell them.'

Roy told half a lie. 'You can still do that, Abel, if you can ride hard and shoot fast, for the balance of this day.'

He did not believe Abel was going to pull through. He thought Jasper might, but he had already decided against Abel, in just about anything. He even considered angling his horse in behind Abel so that when the gunfire erupted, he'd have a human shield. He would not do this, though, not because of any regard he had for Abel, but because he'd seen a horse get shot out from under a man, and the following rider ended up all in a heap, too.

Abel said, 'Yeah; well, if shooting and cussin' and hard-riding will make it possible, why then I'll be down in west Texas come next autumn.' Abel raised a grimy sleeve to squeeze sweat off his face. It was hot enough, now, for that, but it did not *have* to be that kind of sweat. Then Abel rolled a smoke with a flourish, and tilted back his hat as they rode abreast, picking their way eastward exactly as they'd been doing since they had crossed the stageroad a number of miles back, and had entered this strange country of the concave mountainside.

Eastman's cigar got small, but he clung to it, even after it went cold in his mouth. Jasper lifted his hat, once, and re-settled it lower with a hard tug, as though he were preparing himself for the deadly rush shortly to begin for the three of them. Jasper's dun-coloured face looked no different than it had looked before the peril had appeared, except that his sunk-set grey eyes were darker beneath the hat-brim, and he had less to say. He was never really very talkative, and his periods of good-humour were even rarer, but Jasper was a good man to ride the rimrocks with. Roy had thought for a long while now, that Jasper was probably the best man he'd used in his outlaw band since he'd first braced a bank in a cowtown. He would regret it if anything happened to Jasper. That kind were damned hard to find.

The sun was high, the air was clear as glass, and heavy with a tree-sap scent. The land southward, beyond where those parallelling cowboys were riding along, looked richly green for as many miles outward as a man could look. Dakota Territory was good cow-country — except for the killing winters that came every now and then and wiped out herds by the dozens. Maybe, like that clod-hopper Barnard had said, someday it would all be farmed to wheat and oats and such-like. Eastman clamped hard on his cigar. One thing was damned certain; if that day ever arrived, he would not be around to see it, whether he died this afternoon or lived for another five or ten years, and that suited him right down to his bootheels. If there was one kind of person he despised above all others, it was settlers. *He* knew how gawddamned stupid and forlorn and hapless they were, and he despised them with a steady, mindless hatred.

Abel spoke, suddenly. 'You fellers see

anything move up yonder in the trees?'

Roy hadn't even been watching, but he answered because he understood what was happening to Abel. 'Yeah; some bluejays just winged away.'

'Means they're in there, then,' muttered Jasper. 'Camp-robbers been warning folks about other folks ever since I can remember.'

Roy looked at Jasper. 'How long is that?'

Jasper answered without taking his eyes off the nearing forest. 'Twenty-five or twenty-six years. I ain't sure.'

Roy looked at Abel. 'You?'

Abel was annoyed by the question. 'What the hell difference does that make? Twenty-seven years.' Abel turned smouldering pale eyes. 'You, Roy?'

Eastman smiled gently into the younger man's stormy eyes. 'Fifty-one. And I can do anything at fifty-one I could do at fifty.' Eastman laughed. The other two smiled at him, then, when Eastman took a fresh hold of his reins, they all exchanged another, different kind of look.

The trees were only about a half mile ahead. If there were dismounted men in among them, with Winchesters, the outlaws were almost in fair carbine range.

Roy, still with the cigar stub clamped

tight, said, 'You boys ready?'

They were. 'Ready as I'll ever be,' replied Abel, and Jasper did not speak, he simply eased his right hand to the gun-stock on his right thigh, and waited for Eastman to gouge his horse with the spurs.

Chapter Fourteen

A FIGHT FOR LIFE!

Eastman made a final appraisal of their condition. The men behind them were still there, strung out up and down the slope, and although they were gaining a little, they were not doing it very fast. Possibly they were not supposed to, or else they did not want to make a rush at three armed, desperate outlaws.

There was another possibility which crossed Eastman's mind. If there were ambushers ahead in the forest, and if a fight started, stray slugs aimed at the outlaws could very easily reach far enough back to empty a few saddles among those allies of the men up ahead.

In any case, Roy Eastman did not view those men behind them as an immediate threat. As for the men on the south range, the only benefit they could be to their friends would be in the event the Eastman gang turned away from the confrontation in the forest, and tried to escape down-country, and that idea crossed Eastman's mind, too. There were probably fewer men on the south range than anywhere else. But that was a guess, and regardless of whether it was valid or not, if the outlaws could reach the trees, they would have an entire forest to utilize as protective background.

He weighed it well and decided that a frontal break for the forest was their best chance. He looked at the younger men and said, 'We're about in bushwhacking range. You fellers ready?'

They were.

The mountainside curved back around, again; they had ridden deep across its concave face and were now swinging towards the thick-bulking continuation. Eastman said, 'Colts, boys, not Winchesters,' and reached down with his clawing right hand as he also took a deep seat in the saddle. *Let's go!'*

They hooked their startled horses and lit down in a flinging rush. The land was brushy and there were still a few trees around and ahead of them, but it did not slope southward so much from here until they reached the trees, so, except for the times when their fired-up mounts had to leap over deadfall-trees or thickets of thorny brush, they had a clear run dead ahead.

For about a hundred feet nothing happened except that someone down on the south range let off a high shout which struck the mountainside and bounced back with a high echo, then two gunshots sounded, but from far back, not in front of them. Eastman had time to wonder with rising hope whether there actually was anyone ahead of them, so far the activity had come from the rear, and off on their right, but that was only a brief hope.

The men ahead in the trees finally overcame their surprise, or whatever had held them back once the outlaws broke and ran for it. A snarling, flat-sounding carbine-shot came from the onward forest. Eastman, riding loose and easy in the saddle, aimed at the smoke-puff and fired his sixgun. Abel did the same, but he thumbed off a second shot. Jasper was riding low on his horse's back, concentrating on reaching the trees.

A second and third gunshot broke from up in the trees. Roy heard one of those slugs sing past, low. The ambushers were not aiming at the men, they were trying to down their horses.

The forest loomed close. Ragged gunfire flashed from several directions. Eastman's detachment allowed him to estimate to himself that there were only three or four men on ahead. But they were invisible in the forest, and they did not remain stationary; once a man fired he stepped quickly away to find another place to fire from. Maybe this was the reason none of the outlaws or their horses were struck.

The gunfire from far back abruptly stopped as the pursuing eight or ten horsemen back there ceased firing, probably because of fear they might inadvertently strike their allies up ahead. Whatever the reason, it worked in the favour of the fleeing outlaws. They only had to face those three or four men dead ahead, and because these men fired, then hastily moved clear, their bullets only occasionally even came close.

Roy's powerful seal-brown horse reached the first thick stand of trees. From here on it was each man for himself. Roy had already decided he would go uphill, not straight ahead nor southward. It would use up his horse fast, flinging up a mountainside, but this was exactly why he rode a powerful, sound animal; so that in a real pinch he would have that little extra that might keep him alive. When it got to the place where he'd have to abandon the worn-out animal, he might, with some luck, have gained enough ground to be reasonably safe.

He did not look around to see where Jasper and Abel were, once he flashed past the first crowded stand of pines. He strained to see the ambushers around him, and once he glimpsed a man standing exposed with his Winchester snugged back and tilted to fire. Roy dropped down the off-side of his horse as the man fired — and missed. Then the horse side-stepped around a huge tree and Roy hauled himself back into the saddle, twisting to fire back. But the man was lost in the forest.

Colts sounded, finally, during this period of close infighting. He thought Jasper was boring directly ahead, eastward, from the sounds of the gunfire, perhaps with Abel trying to keep up with him, but it was impossible to see much because he had to also concentrate on not being knocked senseless by low limbs as his panicked horse ducked and dodged around the close-spaced trees.

The gunfire swelled furiously as those eight or ten pursuers from farther back finally burst into the forest too. Men shouted excitedly back and forth, their bellowing punctuated by furious exchanges of deafening, slamming sixgun-fire.

In a calm moment Eastman might have reflected on the fact that those men who had been waiting in ambush among the trees had been more concerned with their own safety and survival, than with actually bringing down the Eastman gang, otherwise any one of them would have realized that the same trees which protected them also offered protection to their prey. But the instinct to survive was strong. Also, not many rangemen, and even fewer townsmen, were anxious to trade shots with professional outlaws, men who lived by their guns.

Actually, all Eastman had time to think about during the fight, was the trees; not the gunshots, because if a slug found him he probably wouldn't know it, but the damned trees were twice as large around as a man, and they stood so close in some places a horse had difficulty swinging past, around, and through, them all.

Somewhere a horse screamed, then went silent. Several men called back and forth, and the ragged gunfire seemed not to diminish so much as it seemed to change both in pattern and direction. The possemen were running eastward now, firing both carbines and beltguns as they turned off from the direction Eastman was taking, up the slope northeasterly.

He wanted to save his animal. It had been his second-nature for too many years and under too many trying circumstances, for him not to think of it now, but the horse was running mindlessly, and Eastman allowed him to do it even though it appeared, for the time being at any rate, that he had burst through the possemen and was now, seconds later, beyond them and escaping, and therefore did not need all that power and haste.

They reached a circular, grassy clearing. Here, when the seal-brown would have rushed straight out into the open, Eastman exerted the first rein-pressure since he'd kicked out his horse; he forced the animal to veer, to continue on through the trees up past the clearing.

The gunfire sounded muffled and distant, finally, and this was when Eastman finally hauled his horse down, but by then the animal's rib-cage was pumping like an over-worked bellows, he was only about a half mile away from being wind-broke.

Eastman did not climb any further, to favour the horse, instead he turned due eastward and walked the horse on a level course for a solid hour. By the end of this time he did not hear any gunfire back down the mountain anywhere.

It was hot in among the trees even though no sunlight reached past the bristle-coned, high tops of this particular segment of the forest. Hot and breathless, and the seal-brown was dripping water as he plugged along head-hung tired. If they had to run again, the horse wouldn't be able to keep it up for very long and Eastman knew it. But he did not stop to rest the horse for the best of all reasons; the surest way to chest-founder an overheated mount was to stop and let him stand perfectly still while breathing in great amounts of upland air. The best cure now, was to keep him moving, which Eastman did, and which he would have done regardless, because danger was still close. Eastman had no illusions about *that*.

The ominous silence back down the slope where the fight had taken place could mean one of two things; either Jasper and Abel had been caught back there, and shot, or else they had escaped, with almost twenty men beating the countryside in search of them. Either way, nothing was really settled.

Someone would be on Eastman's track too. The only compensating factor, to Eastman's way of thinking, was that whoever he was — or whoever *they* were — their horses would not be in much better shape than his horse was in.

It took a full hour for the horse to stop his laboured breathing. Afterwards, though, he still plugged along, head-hung, dragging his feet. He would recover, by sundown, but he would be tuckered up and tired for a long time yet to come, for days in fact, unless Eastman could find a hiding place so the horse could rest, and even then, without grain and hard feed, the horse was not going to fully recover. Grass was fine for animals to grow fat on, but it wasn't worth a damn for animals being used hard.

Otherwise, though, Roy Eastman's confidence returned a little at a time as hours passed without there being any sounds of either pursuit behind him, or gunfire elsewhere down the mountainside. He talked to the horse, which was the custom among men who spent more time among animals than among people, or who liked the company of animals the best. He told the horse that evidently the Eastman legend was supposed to acquire another vivid story of a miraculous escape.

The sun slanted, eventually, and the horse's gait picked up a little. Eastman did not try for the top-out, although he would have liked to because, once he got beyond these mountains, he would be in distant, new country again. He had to favour the horse, but as he watched the skyline come and go through the trees on his left, he thought he might try getting over the rimrocks tomorrow, and head northward.

Generally, the country was mountainous for hundreds of miles, if a man chose not to descend to the immense plains and plateaus, which marked the country between the Dakotas and Montana. If Eastman could have a week's respite, they would not even know where to look for him, and if they were tracking him, since riders could not make a race of it in the mountains, and since he already had a fair head-start, the chances of them overtaking him would grow less and less as the days passed.

But somewhere he was going to have to leave the seal-brown in a pasture and steal a fresh horse, something he would regret. It was not altogether that he liked the seal-brown, although that was indeed a consideration, it was more practically that ranch-horses were rarely ever as bred-up for power and endurance and strength. He would be trading 'down' but that could not be avoided now. The seal-brown had done his best, and now he had to have rest and decent food.

The sun continued to slant away, the warmth in the forest began to lessen slightly, the shadows deepened, and finally Roy Eastman punched out all the spent casings from his Colt and re-loaded, then holstered the gun and leaned to look his horse and saddle over for injuries. There were scratches from limbs and underbrush, but not a single bullet-burn.

His linen duster, though, was ripped and torn at the hem, and part way up the back, probably as a result of being snagged by underbrush. He removed it, balled it up and flung it away, and finally, the let-down reached him. He began to feel almost as weary and dispirited as his horse felt. What ultimately helped mitigate this natural condition was the bulge in his trouser pockets. He patted that, felt something and glanced down. He *had* been hit, after all; there was a neat, small hole, evidently made by a Winchester slug because it was too small for a Colt's bullet, directly through his trouser pocket. The bullet had ploughed through the wadded money too. Instead of taking out some of the notes to examine them, he told the horse that, by gawd, the money had saved him from being hit in the thigh, and *that* sure as hell was a miracle. He even smiled about it.

Chapter Fifteen

PURSUIT!

Eastman did not stop until the moon was high and he had to halt or the seal-brown was going to quit him.

His camp was in a small glade where there was a spring and good grass, although not much grass, actually, because the glen was so small. He off-saddled with aching muscles. The horse did not eat right away, he simply stood wide-legged and head-hung.

Eastman ate a little of the food taken from the cache, and afterwards wished he'd had a cigar. Finally, fearing to build a fire even though he felt sure he was entirely alone in the forest, he rolled into his blankets. Sleep came so quickly he hardly had time to wonder about Jasper and Abel.

When he awakened the seal-brown gelding was cropping grass within a foot of his head. That sound had brought his eyes wide open; it sounded almost as though someone were trying to sneak up on him. He lay with a pounding heart until he saw the horse, heard him, then the sense of relief was delicious and Eastman did not move for a full ten minutes.

There was soft light over against the far treetops, visible from his fen, and the cold was not as bad as he expected. The reason for that, he saw when he finally rolled out, stiff in every muscle, was because the sky was building up with a high overcast. There was the scent of rain in the high-country air.

He arose, washed at the spring, ate cold tinned peaches, wished again for a smoke, and finally went over to remove the horse's hobbles. The animal was tucked up in the flank, but his eyes were clear and he was alert. How long this fresh energy would last was not much in doubt, and Eastman knew it as he lugged up the saddle and rigged his animal out.

When they left the glen Eastman began angling towards the top-out. He utilized game-trails, which never went straight up a mountain, but which wound around back and forth, gaining elevation a little at a time. It was easier on the horse, and also on the man.

By the time they were near the top, Eastman paused for a rearward look. Below and behind him, the mountainside slanted thickly away, southward, and on both sides. He saw a diffusing layer of smoke far down the slope, near the foothills and the farther plain. He smiled about that; whoever they were, they were miles away. He turned for the last hundred yards and when the trees thinned out, where wintry blasts had bent and twisted the few bristle-top pines brave enough to try and exist up here, he had a good view on all sides. Just short of the rimrocks, he thought he'd caught movement off on his left, to the west, and not very far below, and rode up beside a tree to halt and sit motionless for a moment.

Three horsemen were coming, picking their way without haste. Something wadded and tied behind one of those saddles held Eastman's attention. Then he swore aloud. 'Gawddammit; my duster!'

They were undoubtedly excellent trackers. Good enough to keep on his trail even after nightfall, and *that* was something not even many Indians would have been able to do. But of course these men had probably had help from the other possemen; they would have known, for example, that since Eastman had not broken away southward, and could not have continued on eastward without great peril, he'd had to try for the rimrocks.

He rode away from the tree, across a clearing heading for the rims, and when he got up there he did not even try to find a low slot to pass over, through, which normally a hunted man would have done, because now the chase was not going to depend upon his ability to hide, it was going to depend upon his wiliness at using up his horse to his own best advantage, and that was *all* this chase would depend upon.

Across the mountaintop lay another wooded slope. He angled the seal-brown down it without even looking back, but this side of the mountain was not as wooded, nor as thick-bulking as the opposite side, and below, stretching away towards some tin-topped structures in the middle distance, which would be a town, was a huge plateau, a great plain of grasslands which could not be avoided unless Eastman turned eastward or westward. He dared not risk the westerly course, and if he turned along the eastward slope, he was going to use up his horse and end upon foot. He headed straight down towards the plain.

The sun came and went as great grey clouds floated across an expanse of sky which was endlessly curved and troubled. One moment sunshine struck those tin roofs, the next moment they lay leaden, as drab as the underbelly of a fish.

He paused mid-way down and listened,

but the men back there were not riding fast nor recklessly, so they did not make loud sounds. He went almost down to the level country and dismounted, left his horse in a hidden place, took his carbine and hiked back a half mile hoping to catch sight of the riders. This time, although he did not see them, he heard loose shale slide under shod hooves. They were gaining, which meant they were having no trouble keeping to his trail now, in daylight. It also meant that their animals were not worn out.

He returned to the seal-brown, swung up, leathered his Winchester and rode directly out to the level country, then he had to turn, that, or ride out into open country where they could see him very easily.

He turned westerly against his better judgement, but with a desperate plan forming in his mind. There was a stageroad over there, somewhere, he knew for a fact, but it was probably miles distant. In any case, he had to reach it, had to find a stage or a wagon, or even a freighter, before he hung his saddle, blanket and bridle in a tree, said good-bye to the seal-brown horse, and tried to escape in a way his pursuers probably would not expect.

The horse had used up his renewed energy crossing the mountain, and now, down where he had easier going, he hung in the bit a little, and dragged his feet again.

Where the trees had been cut, probably to furnish building and heating wood for that tin-topped town he had seen in the distance, grass grew abundantly among the slash, and the rotting stumps, and here, at least, the sidehill was not very steep. Someone ran cattle up here, as well as out a distance upon the plateau. Eastman knew the kind; they were called stump-ranchers because this was the only kind of land they could afford. It brought a small, fresh hope to him as he came on around the slope and saw the log house, low and massive, and the nearby log barn, with its mud-wattling along the front wall, and its chinked great logs on both sides. There was smoke coming from the stone chimney, but what held Roy Eastman's attention were the horses in a pole corral mid-way between the house and the barn. There looked to be six or eight horses; out of that many there was bound to be one strong, rideable animal.

Eastman veered into the trees and began a big circling ride which brought him, eventually, around behind the log house where he was sufficiently screened by un-cut trees to be able to sit his saddle and get a better look at both the yard, and those corralled horses.

It looked as though there were more than one stout young animal in that corral. He ran a soiled hand across bearded lips, stepped off, tied the seal-brown, moved ahead until he was directly behind the house, then stepped forth to make a rush over the cleared land. If he had ridden in, they would have seen him for sure. He would have preferred to ride in, but couldn't take that chance now; he'd go back for his saddle and bridle later, after he had the fresh animal. Moreover, he did not have the time to palaver before getting the drop. Not with those three grimly-stubborn pursuers still coming.

He got to the edge of the house, smelled frying meat and frying potatoes, along with a fresh pot of coffee, and leaned a moment savouring that wonderful combination of fragrances, then he palmed his sixgun and stepped ahead towards the raised, plank porch. He hadn't quite reached it when a man's voice, deep and rough, caught him in the back from the area of the barn.

'Hey! You with the gun in your hand! Don't you take another gawddamned step!'

Eastman halted and very slowly turned, seeking that rough-voiced man. All he saw was the corralled horses, otherwise there was no movement, no silhouette, and no man-shape. But from a squared hole in the south side of the barn a long-barrelled rifle was aiming squarely his way. Eastman holstered his Colt and called back.

'Mister, I ain't got time to talk. I'll pay you five hundred dollars for the best stout young horse you got in the corral.'

The rifle did not move an iota. For a moment there was no response, then it came in the same rough-toned way. 'Will you now. Stranger, if you're in such a hurry that'll mean they's fellers on the trail ahind you. Is that right?'

Eastman glanced across in the direction he had ridden from, as he replied. 'That's right. Five hundred in cash for the house, quick now.'

The rifle still did not droop but this time the rough voice spoke more briskly. 'All right. Count it out, lay it there on the ground, and take that buckskin with the zebra markin's on his legs. He's four years old and tougher'n anything that'll be ahind you. Hurry it up, stranger. I don't want no gunfight here in my yard.'

Eastman hurried for the same reason, *he* did not want a gunfight in this stump-rancher's yard either. As he put the money upon the ground and stuffed the rest of it back into his pocket, the door opened silently behind him and a red-headed, red-bearded, lanky, work-roughened man in his forties stepped forth on stocking feet as silent as an animal. He levelled a cocked Colt and said, 'Mister, put it *all* on the ground.'

Eastman stiffly craned around. He had not expected there might be *two* of them. He and the red-bearded man exchanged a long look, then Eastman fished forth the wadded, crumpled bills and dropped them.

The red-bearded man smiled to show bad teeth and a wad of tobacco in his cheek. 'Go get the buckskin,' he ordered. 'Move fast, mister.'

Eastman moved fast. He did not expect either of those stump-ranch cowmen to shoot him, not when the sound would bring his pursuers on the run and they'd lost their newfound wealth, but most of all, he did not want to waste time being cautious, so he ran to the corral. The man inside the barn came forth with a rope in one hand, his old army rifle in the other hand. He threw the rope to Eastman, who climbed the pole-stringers, talked his way up to the buckskin horse, caught the best and led it towards the corral's rear gate. As he turned to close the gate he saw both those men standing in plain view, guns in hand, watching. He could have killed the one in the barn doorway with one shot, and probably could also have got the other one, over in his stocking-feet on the plank porch. He would have done it, too, almost any other time. Now, he was running for his life — without a red cent to make it worthwhile.

He spun on his heel and led the buckskin over to the trees where the seal-brown stood patiently waiting. It only took a few minutes to adjust the bridle to the new horse, to switch the blanket and the saddle, and to spring up across leather and rein back up through the rearward trees. The seal-brown turned to dutifully follow, but when Eastman cursed at him and flagged him off by waving his hat, the seal-brown horse halted, watched Eastman hurry on his way, then he turned and ambled back in the direction of that corralful of horses over beside the log barn.

Eastman had power and strength under him again. It made a lot of difference in his outlook. He also paused, once, just before leaving the trees for the last time, heading straight out towards that distant town, and scanned the rearward countryside. He did not see his pursuers; they had not yet reached the stump-ranch, which was even more encouraging.

He had no trepidation now, about being seen out on the flat ground. If his pursuers gave chase, he would outrun them easily. They were still riding the same animals they'd ridden the previous day, while Roy Eastman had a bundle of power and soundness under him.

A little trickle of warm rain began falling. For a short while it barely more than settled an occasional drop upon him, but after a quarter of an hour, it began falling more heavily, and by the time Eastman could make out the buildings up ahead, the rain had obscured those mountains behind him.

He was riding across an open land where no one from back there could see him. There was some good, evidently, in every rain that fell — to someone.

Chapter Sixteen

COULTERVILLE

The linen duster would not have helped against that particular downpour, but Eastman wished he'd still had it. He had no poncho, which would have turned the water, so, by the time he could make out the buildings up ahead, he was drenched, his saddleseat was soggy and cold, and even the buckskin horse looked almost dun-coloured from a soaking.

Summer rains were good for the land, for the animals that grazed the land, and also for the upland forests where the sap was running and each summertime hot day increased the very real danger of fire. But welcome as this rain undoubtedly was in most places, by the time Roy Eastman reached the askew wooden sign that announced the town up ahead, with a population of two hundred, was named Coulterville, he was miserable and shaking.

His intention had been to ride in, turn the buckskin loose if he could not sell him quickly for enough to buy fresh clothes and a stage-ticket, then rob someone for spending money, tie and gag them, and when the coach appeared heading north, to continue his flight in this fashion. Ordinarily, this kind of a dismal, wet day would have been ideal for such an undertaking. People stirred very little when it was pelting down rain. Even townspeople hovered close to stoves and dry places.

He did not scout-up the town, either, which he normally would have done, but rode directly into it from the southeast, slogged his way to the liverybarn, which was at the lower end of town, rode under the first decent roof he'd been under in several days, stepped down and when the hostler appeared looking round-eyed at the gaunt, dripping, sunken-eyed, bearded stranger, Eastman handed over the reins, asked where the liveryman was, and when the dayman said his boss was over at the cafe, eating, Eastman nodded and turned away to stand in the doorway where little gusts of a cold, blasting wind tore at him while he squinted through the rain-squall studying the buildings around him. The cafe was lighted and its front roadway window was steamy. Elsewhere, up and down the ram-cowed town, there were window lights. Eastman thought of Christmas, for some reason, then struck out through runnels of chocolaty water for the cafe.

He had to hold himself taut to keep from shaking. Each blast of wind cut through his soaked clothing. Actually, he did not feel particularly cold, he felt warm. In fact, he felt a little warmer than he usually felt. The shakes had to be caused by something else. He had no time to speculate about this. For one thing, he thought those possemen might still be coming, rain or no rain. They would perhaps be delayed at the stump-ranch, but not for very long, so he had to hasten. For another thing, Eastman's mind was filled to capacity with just one driving motivation — to stay free, to keep moving, to survive.

At the cafe there were several men along the counter desultorily talking and drinking coffee. Only two of them were really eating, and the liveryman was one of those. Nor was he difficult to identify; horsetraders, professional horsemen, had a singular stamp. Eastman approached the counter dripping water in rivulets. Several men looked up, and shook their heads. The liveryman stared at Eastman too, as the outlaw straddled the bench beside him, tipped back his head so rainwater would drip off the back of his hat instead of the front, and when the cafeman came, looking mildly annoyed at all that tracked-in mud and water, Eastman asked for hot coffee. Then he spoke to the liveryman.

'I just left a good outfit over at your barn. Young, stout buckskin horse, a sound A-fork saddle, and a good using bridle with a California silver-cheek-pieced half-breed bit.'

The liveryman was a fat man with a moon face and a lot of little sharp features pushed up tight in the centre of it. He stared at Eastman, drank some hot coffee, set the cup down and slowly nodded, having completed his appraisal. 'And you want to peddle the outfit,' he said, quietly, matter-of-factly.

'Yeah.'

The liveryman inclined his head with the same maddening slowness again. 'I reckon it can be done, stranger. Only we got to walk back over there so's I can see what I'm getting.'

The cafeman brought Eastman's coffee, set it down then leaned, looking balefully at the bearded man. Eastman fished out some silver, all he had left, and dropped a coin of it a-top the counter. The cafeman kept solemnly staring, then he said, 'Mister, you better get some hot grub inside you.' He scooped up the small coin. 'While you're guzzling coffee I'll dish you up some hot hash and spuds.' He looked briefly at the liveryman, who looked impassively back, then the liveryman smiled and said, 'Drink up, friend. You're wetter'n a snow-goose.'

The cafeman padded through a hanging blanket into his kitchen, but did not stop there. He grabbed a dowdy old hat, pulled it low and went out the back door of his cafe in a hunched over run, cursing as the wind and water hit him, making him gasp.

The liveryman seemed to be a very deliberate man, but as the warmth worked its way into Roy Eastman, he was content to sit for a short while. It was good just not to be moving, for a change. The cafe was warmed by a popping big old iron stove in a corner, and the coffee did the rest. Gradually, Eastman's muscles loosened. He sighed, leaned on the counter and said, 'That's one hell of a rain out there, mister.'

The liveryman nodded again, slowly and gravely. 'Yep; no sense in a man trying to ride in weather like this. All's he'll do is fetch up with croup or Messican 'flu or some other damned complaint.' He did not look at Roy Eastman, but slowly ate from a large platter. 'You looking for a riding job?' he asked. 'If you are, stranger, you'd better keep the saddle and bridle; cow outfits furnish mounts, but not outfits.'

'Passing through,' murmured Eastman, holding back a paroxysm of the shakes, and afterwards finishing the coffee. 'You got a smoke?'

The liveryman not only had tobacco, he had it in cigar-form, and passed a stogie to Eastman with hardly more than glancing around as he did so. 'Lousy time of the year to be broke,' he commented, stuffing his face, and Eastman offered his detached little smile.

'No time of the year is a good time to be broke,' he replied. 'When's the stage leave Coulterville?'

'Hour, maybe. It come in slippin' and slitherin' this morning, the whip cussing his head off about the condition of the south road.'

A warning sounded in Eastman's head. He put his brown stare upon the liveryman. 'From the south? Did it bring any news, or anything like maybe travellin' pedlars, from down-country?'

The liveryman ran a creased sleeve across his lips, pushed the empty plate away and pulled in his cup of java. He stared directly down into the cup as he replied because he knew for a plain fact that he was one of those unfortunate individuals who just simply could not tell a bald-faced lie without it showing all over his face.

'Only as far as I know, that the lousy rain sure made the road slippery in short order.' He raised the cup and held it not quite to his lips. 'That don't usually happen, especially this time of year; usually, it takes maybe half a day, sometimes even a full day, before the roads get awash.' The liveryman drained his cup, set it resolutely away, and brought forth another cigar, which he took his time lighting. Then, finally, he said, 'Well, mister, if that danged fool don't fetch your meal directly, we'll just have to walk out of here without you eating, because I got a busy day ahead of me.' He blew smoke at the pie-table beyond the counter, then, finally, turned towards Roy Eastman, who was holding his hot cup between both hands. 'About this buckskin horse; mind telling me where you got him?'

Eastman did not mind. 'From some ranchers up yonder against the south slopes.'

The liveryman pondered that; it posed more questions than it supplied answers. For example, why would a man buy a horse, and obviously use up all his money for that purpose, only to ride the beast six or seven miles, then sell it again? Didn't make much sense at all.

'You give a fair price, did you?' he asked, and again Eastman answered truthfully. 'A hell of a lot more'n the bastard is worth, if he'd been made of gold.' Then Eastman put down the coffee cup and looked around as several of the cafe's patrons shuffled out into the wind-driven rainfall, admitting a great gust of chilling cold each time they opened the door.

The storm was not abating, it seemed to be getting worse. The yonder roadway was a shambles, great ruts had been washed every which way, and were chuck-full of swirling, mud-thickened water. The rainfall was coming straight down. It made the inside of the cafe roar with a steady sound. The wind was increasing as well. If those possemen had been imprudent enough to try and reach the town from the foothills, by now they had ought to be riding fetlock-deep through water. If they had no ponchos, either, they were going to be even more soaked and feverish than their prey was.

Eastman smiled to himself; they had probably been at the stump-ranch when the rain arrived, and that would be pretty damned ironic, them sitting up there in the kitchen, probably listening to rain-thunder on the roof, drinking coffee with the men who had all Eastman's share of the Sioux Falls bank robbery, without even knowing those 'honest' cowmen had all that money.

His smile faded. At least they would be dry and warm, up there at the damned sidehill cow outfit.

He walked out of the restaurant with the fat liveryman, and oddly enough, his soggy clothing, which had been drying a little in the hot cafe, had also been storing up more heat than dry clothing could have, and Eastman therefore did not feel the cold, right away. The liveryman looked at him and wagged his head. It was useless to try and speak, because the overhang out front of the cafe was tin-roofed. The rain beating upon that metal awning made a sound like a dozen waterfalls cascading over a dozen cataracts, or like the mind-stunning up-close sound of a great buffalo herd shaking the very earth in a stampede.

The liveryman turned up his jacket-collar, pulled down his old hat, gazed with distaste and some dismay at the great, water-filled cracks in the roadway, then hollered.

'Let's go, stranger. Gawd o'mighty what a rain!'

They struck out and were nearly upset by the first wall of water that gushed around their legs, sucking at them.

Two cowboys standing under an overhang across the way, out front of a saloon, whooped encouragement to them, and laughed as the liveryman and Roy Eastman had to reach for one another to avoid being bowled over. The liveryman's centre of gravity was lower. It was also greater. He made it to the far plank-walk and released Eastman as he flung upwards to stamp on solid wood. Eastman *almost* made it, but when the fat man released his hold, and a freshet of furious force struck Eastman's booted feet, he staggered, fighting to keep his footing, and desperately jammed one leg wide for support — and stepped into a deep hole with that out-flung leg. He windmilled with both arms, lost his balance, struggled furiously to avoid falling sidewards into the mud and water, and won. He fell forward — both arms flung wide, face-first against a log upright supporting an overhang.

A stunning array of brilliant lights exploded inside Eastman's head. He fell forward upon the plankwalk, rolled, flopped over, and blood trickled from his nose as well as from a gash upon his forehead. Those two laughing cowboys suddenly went silent.

Chapter Seventeen

EASTMAN'S FINAL 'ESCAPE'

Five men stood in the log jailhouse with three of them attired in long black riders' ponchos dripping water in great circles around where they stood. The other man, wearing a water-logged disreputable old hat and a flour-sack apron made fast around his thick girth with a length of binder-twine, stood with his back to the merrily popping stove, while the fifth man, with a badge upon his shirtfront, leaned against a cluttered old battered desk as he said, 'Yeah; we heard about it this morning when the stage reached town, but I sure-Lord had no idea any of them could possibly get this far in that little time.' He looked at Jack Moses, the Town Constable from Sioux Falls. 'I guess it'll be him all right. Jerry here, the cafeman, got the description from that stage driver over breakfast coffee. You heard what he just run up here to tell me.'

Constable Moses nodded. The two men with him, Will Billings from the plundered bank, and the other man, cowhide-booted, pale and troubled, Joshua Barnard, said nothing until the constable jerked a thumb in their direction.

'They'd both know him on sight. This here feller works in the bank; he was right there when them bastards walked in waving guns. This other one — he's a settler north-west of Sioux Falls — Eastman put up with him for a few days before they met in town and raided us. He'd recognize him too.' Jack Moses reached to mop water off his chin. He and the town constable of Coulterville looked steadily at one another, an unasked, an unanswered, question, lying between them. There was the matter of a legal apprehension; you got into all sorts of trouble just sashaying up and jamming a gun into someone's ribs.

Constable Moses stepped forward to the desk, unhooked his shiny poncho and plunged a hand deep inside. As he brought it forth and dropped the crumpled greenbacks a-top the desk he said, 'This here is one third of the loot stolen from our bank in Sioux Falls. Look at it, Constable; you want to know how we come to take it away from those two stump-ranchers up there? Because that, right there, is a bullet-hole smack-dab through the whole bundle of it, and when those lyin' stump-ranchers seen it, they didn't know what to say. So I and my friends here, sort of convinced them to try telling the truth.' Moses watched Coulterville's lawman lean to examine the smashed, worn banknotes, and when the cafeman edged in to also look, Constable Moses said, 'Eastman made one special mistake. He abandoned his seal-brown horse, because it was rode-down, and when we walked into the yard, there it come, walking across from the direction of the yonder trees, still wet with saddle-sweat. The horse was just looking for other horses. There was some in the stump-ranchers' corral. That was what convinced us immediately, so we got down and got to talking to those lyin' bastards up there . . . I think they might have fought us, if they'd dared. Anyway, they're chained to the stove in their kitchen, whenever you want to go back and get them. We put the seal-brown horse in the barn. We'll take him back with us for evidence.' Jack Moses reached to pick up the wadded money, which was also legal evidence.

Coulterville's lawman straightened back. 'How much is there?'

'Four thousand dollars,' replied Moses, jamming the money back into a trouser-pocket.

'You get the rest of it? We heard over here

they got twelve thousand. Lord, but that's an awful lot of money, Mr Moses.'

The Sioux Falls lawman smiled thinly. 'It's a lot of money, Mr Horning, for a damned fact, and yes, we got the rest of it. Like I was telling you before this here gent from the cafe come busting in, we almost had them cornered on the east slope up above Fargo, but they guessed who we were and there was a hell of a fight. The other two got killed. We got their horses first, then we cornered them too, and fought it out to a fare-thee-well. Each one of them had another four thousand in his pants.' Constable Moses looked out of the window where the rain was beating with the unrelenting force of a thousand tiny fists. When he glanced back he said, 'The cafeman said Eastman went to the liverybarn. Well; you care to come along, Mr Horning, or not?'

Coulterville's town constable did not answer. He did not look very happy either, but he went to a wall-peg for his hat, his gunbelt, and his poncho. While he donned these things he said, 'Jerry; you stay in here until I get back.'

The cafeman offered absolutely no protest. The expression on his face, in fact, suggested that he could not have been driven to accompany the others with an ox goad.

They walked out into the wind and rain, milled for a moment as the water struck, stinging their faces, then hunched their backs and turned southward with the squall beating upon their black-coated backs. The Coulterville constable walked abreast, with Jack Moses from Sioux Falls. Behind those two came troubled Joshua Barnard and grim-faced Will Billings. Those four were the only people in the roadway from one end of town to the other end.

When they had almost reached the liverybarn, the fat liveryman came hurrying on up, wearing a poncho too, his face speckled with rainwater. He ignored everyone but the Coulterville lawman and gushed words in a strong shout because he was facing into the squall as he spoke.

'Hey, Paul; Jerry get to tell you who we got in town? I was walking across the road with him, and — right over yonder — he stepped in a chuck-hole and fell forward, crackin' his face upon that log upright. Knocked him colder'n a block of ice. I took the gun off him, Paul, and right now and here, I'm servin' notice I want a piece of the reward. You hear me?'

Jack Moses leaned, looked stonily at the fat man. 'Where is he, mister; what'd you do with him?'

'Got two rangeriders to lend me a hand and hauled him up to doc's office.' The liveryman raised a rubber-sleeved arm, pointing. 'Yonder, gents, where the light shows.'

Coulterville's lawman turned on his heel and jerked his head at the others without speaking. Not until they had bucked the storm as far northward as they'd previously travelled southward, and could huddle near the lighted window and doorway of a small slab-building, did he attempt to speak. He put his lips up close to Moses' ear and said, 'Somebody better go round back. There's two ways out of this place.'

Constable Moses reached under his dripping raincoat and palmed his Colt. He looked back and motioned for Billings and Barnard to do the same. They did. Then Jack Moses answered the other lawman. 'You just open that damned door, Constable, and get out of the way. If that son of a bitch is in there, he ain't going to make it out any back door, or any other door, for that matter.'

Moses gestured, Constable Horning hesitated a moment, gazing from a cold face at Constable Moses, then he shrugged and turned doorward. If these damned fools from Sioux Falls wanted to get themselves killed, that was their business. He stepped up, grasped the knob, gave it a wrenching twist and heaved the door so far back it struck the wall with the sound of a gunshot. Wind and rain rushed through, behind the men in shiny black raincoats and almost put out two table-lamps that were standing on a table behind the far window.

A small, wizened man appeared angrily in an adjoining doorway. He glared at the younger, larger men, then snapped at them to close the door, which Will Billings did, and leaned against it, gun in hand, as the Coulterville constable stepped up and peered beyond the small, older man, into the room beyond. The older man said, 'Paul, what in tarnation are you doing; put up that damned gun!'

Jack Moses stepped up and also peered into the adjoining room. There was a man in there, lying on a cot. The Sioux Falls constable recognized that bearded face, and gestured for Billings and Barnard to come over. When they obeyed, and also saw the man on the cot, Barnard said, 'That's him, Mr Moses. That's Johnson.'

Moses stepped roughly past the doctor and approached the cot where the brown-eyed man gazed up without any change in expression. Before Moses could speak, Roy

Eastman said, 'Just explain one thing to me; how in hell did you fellers know we was up there on that curved-in sidehill?'

Jack Moses lowered his handgun. 'They got two pigeon clubs, one in Sioux Falls, one over in the Fargo country. The day you raided our bank, those pigeon-fellers sent the message to their friends over near Fargo. They made up a couple of posses over there and headed north for the hills, in case you boys come that way.'

Eastman stared. 'Pigeons . . . ?'

The wizened man stepped over and pointed. 'Out. I don't give a damn if you're the President of the United States, mister, you go back out front into the other room. This man is my patient, and he's ill.'

Jack Moses looked down. 'Got bumped in the face,' he growled, and the old man glowered upwards.

'Bump in the face, like hell. This here man . . .' The doctor turned. 'Constable Horning, what is this all about?'

The Coulterville lawman answered quietly, gazing at the shivering man on the cot. 'Doc, that man is Roy Eastman. He raided the Sioux Falls bank the other —'

The doctor's eyes flew wide. 'Eastman . . . the outlaw?'

'Yes. And doc, these gents are the law

from Sioux Falls with a warrant to arrest him and take him back.'

The doctor faced Jack Moses again. 'Take him back . . . ? Gentlemen, if you'll wait three, four days, you can take him back.' The doctor turned. He and Roy Eastman exchanged a look before the doctor spoke again. 'I'll say it again; this man only has one good lung, and it's filling up. He's got influenza. There is absolutely nothing I can do, except make him easy.' He glanced at the men from Sioux Falls. 'You understand what I mean?'

Eastman offered his detached, impersonal smile to Constable Moses. 'I never knew a man could die without knowing he was about to do it, did you, Constable? Well . . . looks like you won the chase after all. Only now you got to sit around Coulterville three or four days before I go back with you.'

Moses put up his sixgun. He studied the doctor's bleak expression, studied Eastman's feverish, detached smile, then looked at the others and found softness in only one face, that of Joshua Barnard, before he said, 'Doctor, you plumb certain?'

The small, older man stiffened. 'I'm sure. I'm as sure as over fifty years of handling them like this can make me. Now clear out of here.'

They all returned to the front room, and out there the doctor added one more thing. 'I don't see how he managed to keep going as long as he did, to be frank with you, but it's all gone now, all his strength and resistance. So just go down to the saloon and tank up so's you boys don't catch cold too, and then — just wait. Roy Eastman has robbed his last bank and ridden his last escape.'

'Three, four days?' asked Moses, again.

The doctor shook his head. 'Two days at the most, but it won't do any harm letting him think he's got an extra day or two.'

The men from Sioux Falls filed out of the little warm building, along with Coulterville's lawman, and did exactly as the doctor had suggested, they went down to the saloon.